# THE CHRISTMAS CABIN

## A HOLIDAY HOUSE NOVEL

J.L. JARVIS

D1534595

BOOKBINDER PRESS

THE CHRISTMAS CABIN
A Holiday House Novel
J.L. Jarvis
Copyright © 2016 J.L. Jarvis
All Rights Reserved

Published by Bookbinder Press

Print Edition ISBN: 978-0-9906476-8-3
Ebook Edition ISBN: 978-0-9906476-7-6

# ONE

Abbie Harper wound her way through the crowded walkway as shop lights began to glow in the settling dusk. In an hour, New York's Bryant Park would resemble a life-sized Christmas village, with clear glass kiosks aglow with holiday lighting, and shop after shop offering comfort food and hot drinks for meandering shoppers.

Phone to ear, Abbie said, "I can't see you. Oh— there you are!" She promptly waved as she spied Taylor Hillman sitting alone at a table near the ice skating rink.

Abbie plopped down on the wood slat chair and wrinkled her brow. "I'm so sorry I'm late. You shouldn't have waited for me."

"Part of the joy of indulging in Max Brenner's hot

chocolate is sharing the guilt with someone you love." Taylor grinned and stood up. "Save my seat."

"Wait." Abbie dug through her bag for her wallet.

"I got this." And Taylor was gone.

With a quick glance at her messages and email, Abbie tucked her phone back into her valise then pulled out the brief she'd spent all afternoon writing. She made some notes in the margins and exhaled as she crossed out several sentences, then scribbled a few words to insert.

"You're still working?"

Abbie looked up to find Taylor was back with two cups in her hands. Abbie shuffled the papers together and tucked them back into her bag.

"Wait, hold that thought," Taylor said, sitting down. "Ready?" They both took a sip of hot chocolate and sighed in unison.

"That taste is a Christmas miracle," Abbie said as she leaned back and closed her eyes for a moment.

Taylor looked about at the holiday lights with eyes that shone nearly as much—until her eyes settled on Abbie's satchel. "So what's with the papers? You do know we're off for the holidays, right?"

Abbie rolled her eyes. "Bradley dropped it on my desk just before lunch—a case I know nothing about— and he asked me to write a brilliant brief—yes, he said 'brilliant'—and have it on his desk by the end of today."

Taylor curled her upper lip. "And by 'end of today,' he meant—"

"No, no—not the work day, if that's what you're thinking, 'cause that was never going to happen."

"But it's Christmas Eve *Eve*." Taylor practically pouted.

Abbie lifted her eyes and leveled a look at her best friend and shrugged. "If I want to make partner..."

Taylor looked at her with empathy but said nothing. There was nothing she could say. She and Abbie had started at the firm together, fresh out of their respective law schools, but Taylor had made partner last year, while Abbie was still slogging along as an associate. Abbie couldn't disagree with the firm. Taylor was perfect—smart, charming, and also gorgeous. When she walked into a room, it took mere minutes before she was surrounded by people, through no effort or awareness on her part. How could anyone not enjoy being around her? She was fun and clever—and brilliant under pressure. She deserved her success. On top of it all, she was everything Abbie could want in a friend. Their friendship was one of the few things Abbie had not had to work hard for. They had met on their first day at work and had been there for each other ever since.

Taylor took another sip of hot chocolate and

savored the moment. After a sigh, she said, "So you're not going on the cruise with your parents?"

"Parents, as in my mother and step-father? No, Team Mom and Doug are a lot to take at any time of year—but at Christmas? Nope." She shook her head and made a face that drew a good laugh from Taylor. "Besides, a cruise is not Christmas for me, so—just no, I'm not going. I thanked them profusely for inviting me, but I think they were secretly happy it worked out this way. Now they can slobber all over each other's faces without the buzzkill of my spewing up yesterday's breakfast."

Taylor shrugged. "You could blame it on motion sickness."

Abbie lifted a brow. "I guess so. There is motion involved, and it does make me sick."

Taylor laughed, but with sympathy in her eyes. "Why don't you come home with me for Christmas in Harlem with my family? You know they love you."

"And I love them. I'll never forget my first Christmas in New York. Your family was so kind to me —and that brownstone—evergreens wound down the banister, candles, a fire—it was perfect!" Abbie smiled. Since then, Taylor's family had treated her like part of their family—sometimes more than her own. She tried not to dwell on that. "Maybe when I get back I'll stop by, if they'll still have me."

Taylor's brow creased. "So you're going to do it?"

Abbie gave a confident nod. "Yes, I've rented a cabin, and I'm going."

"Alone?"

"Yes," Abbie said brightly. She pulled out her phone and tilted it so Taylor could see. "Look at this. It's greeting card perfect."

Taylor shook her head slowly. "It is pretty, but it's so remote."

"I know! Isn't it perfect? If anyone from the office tries to reach me, there won't be a signal—at least that's my story, and I'm sticking to it."

"What if you need to reach somebody?"

"I won't. But if I do, I'm sure there'll be some sort of phone—probably with a hand crank and an ear piece."

Taylor studied her friend with concern. "Well, if you get lonely up there in your Christmas cabin, you can always change your mind and come to my house."

Abbie set down her empty cup. "Thank you. I'll keep that in mind."

"The offer's open. Just think of me as your back-up plan." Taylor offered a caring smile.

It was growing dark as they emerged from the park and merged with the people walking briskly along the crowded sidewalk on their way home from work. The park was beginning to look its most magical. The two women hugged, exchanged Christmas wishes, and parted ways.

Abbie had taken a few steps when Taylor called out and pointed in the opposite direction. "Are you lost? You live that way."

Abbie winced. "He wants a hard copy on his desk."

"God forbid he'd have to print it himself."

Abbie shrugged. "It's okay. If I took the file home, I'd have to return it before I left. So, this way, I can finish and walk away for a week."

"And when's that going to happen?"

Abbie shrugged. "I've just got a little more work to do."

Taylor nodded. "A little more work. That means—what—ten, eleven o'clock tonight?"

Abbie gave her a look of mixed sadness and guilt. "If I'm lucky."

Taylor's eyes narrowed. "Get some sleep before you start driving tomorrow."

"I will." She gave Taylor another hug. "Merry Christmas."

Taylor grasped Abbie's shoulders and looked at her sternly. "You, too. And promise me you'll call if you have second thoughts."

Abbie smiled. "Thanks, Taylor. I won't, but it's nice to know you'd be there if I did."

With one more round of holiday wishes, they

parted. Abbie turned toward the office, while Taylor headed for the subway that would take her home.

At least one of them could begin their holiday. Once more, Abbie was reminded of how she'd always had to work harder to get what she wanted, like the little kid pedaling fast to keep up with the big kids. She couldn't help it—she didn't like it, but she did it. She'd built her life, such as it was, on hard work and deferred gratification. Currently on the deferred list were, one, making partner at the law firm and, two, having a life.

With a sigh, she rounded the corner just in time to see Bradley Maguire—*dammit*—walk out of the building. She ducked into a shadowy storefront while he tossed his silky blond hair in the wind and went to the curb, where he raised his starched cuff into the air, and a taxi appeared out of nowhere just for him, so it seemed. Abbie sighed. Crisis averted. She just wasn't in the mood for another round of "Merry Christmas—and enjoy toiling away at the work I just dumped on your desk."

Bradley Effing Maguire (or FM, as she and Taylor called him—a code name just in case they were ever overheard grumbling about him in the office) had been her first and last ever fling—office or otherwise. (She was not good at casual sex.) And now he was her boss. That wasn't too awkward.

THEY'D BEEN WORKING on a case together, and FM—well, back then he was Brad—had just won. They went out to a neighborhood bar with some others to celebrate, and the celebration had dwindled down to the two of them. Until then, there had been some sexual tension between them—a lingering glance here and there, a shared moment while they pored over a document a little too closely. A few drinks and the thrill of their legal win brought it up to the surface, like scum on a pond.

He'd been talking. He was always the one doing most of the talking. The man knew his strengths, listening not being among them. But this one time, he just stopped. His eyes locked on hers, and everything grew still. He leaned closer. They kissed. And then the room exploded—or was that her ovaries?—with music and motion. He paid the check and helped her don her coat, and before the hour was up, they were out of a cab and inside her tiny apartment, ripping each other's clothes off like you see in the movies. A few hours later, he kissed her on the forehead and left —like a vampire that couldn't be caught in the daylight (with her). And that was the beginning and end of the affair.

The next day, FM cornered her in the hallway

with his signature smile and said, "Let's not make this awkward."

That was a sure guarantee that it was going to be.

FM glanced up while two people walked out of a room and headed the opposite way down the hall. With the coast once again clear, he said, "Look, it happened. But we have to work together, you know? We're both grownups. There's no reason we can't move on from here."

Of course Abbie nodded and shrugged. Of course.

And they did. He moved on as though nothing had happened, and she moved on, wincing whenever she recalled that it had.

Everyone had regrets, Abbie reminded herself, so this deep stomach churning and gnawing was perfectly normal. Doing stupid things was just part of life. So she'd add this to a file drawer marked Never Again and then try to confine all future thoughts on the topic to that drawer.

AT 9:17 P.M.—WELL ahead of Taylor's prediction, thank you very much—Abbie saved the legal brief to the cloud then printed and aligned the page edges into a perfect stack, attached a binder clip, and set the legal brief and the accordion case file on FM's desk, front

and center. With a satisfied sigh, she then walked through the glass doorway with her chin high and her shoulders eased of their burden of work—for a few days, at least.

Outside, the lit storefronts and streets looked magical as she made her way along the twenty-five blocks to her apartment. She called this "going to the gym," since she didn't have the time or inclination to work out.

She lived in a tiny renovated efficiency apartment. This was real estate secret code. Each time a New York City apartment building was renovated, the apartments were subdivided like some sort of residential mitosis. By midcentury, people would be living in something akin to MRI tubes. It was just a theory, but a viable one. Abbie's apartment had hardwood floors and a large window that looked out at a larger brick wall next door. Sunlight sometimes made its way in on bright, sunny mornings.

Once home, she locked the two dead bolt locks then slipped out of her clothes and into a large, worn-out tee shirt. Nine hours later, which included a rare thing called sleep, she was up, packed, and in a rental car crossing over the Henry Hudson Bridge on her way to her perfect Christmas Cabin in the Adirondack Mountains of upstate New York.

## TWO

Down the winding road overshadowed by trees, Abbie drove, catching occasional glimpses of a river with rocks jutting out of the sparkling water. The mountains towered above, imposing and timeless. She pulled over to the side and got out to stretch her legs. The water rushed along, parallel to the road. Abbie walked down to the edge and breathed in the scent of fresh pines. She felt serene, a feeling she'd almost forgotten. She sighed and went back to the car.

As she continued on her way, she kept her eye out for snow, but there was none yet. There'd been no snow all season, but Abbie was still holding out hope for a white Christmas. She pulled into the small town near the cabin's location and parked in front of a convenience store.

"We're closing in fifteen minutes," said the clerk.

Even the clerks looked happier here. Abbie grabbed some essentials she couldn't bring from the city: ice cream, a bag of ice cubes, and a coffee. Then she ducked into the shop next door just in time to stock up on more wine—as an emergency backup in case she ran out or a trespassing raccoon figured out how a corkscrew worked. Those little beasts were clever.

She loaded the grocery bag into her car, buckled up, and took a sip of fresh coffee while she checked the directions again. Good. She couldn't be more than ten minutes away from the cabin. She pulled onto the road and was approaching an intersection when some jerk in an old pickup truck hit his horn repeatedly while he proceeded to run the stop sign. Abbie slammed on the brakes and watched, stunned. Had she not been alert to his honking, she might not have made it to Christmas. Although, to be honest, his honking was loud enough to alert the whole county. But still, the man ran a stop sign! Where did he think he was, New York City?

She rolled down the window and offered the pickup driver a personalized holiday greeting. After a few grunts of exasperation, Abbie took a deep cleansing breath and felt better. *Only ten minutes to tranquility,* she reminded herself. Thirty minutes and a few wrong turns later, she pulled into the long dirt driveway that led to the cabin. Making a mental note that a GPS wouldn't work where there wasn't a signal, she resolved to pick up an old-school paper map the next time she was in town.

She parked the car and stared. Here it was, just like the picture. She'd learned to hope for little and expect even less, which always made for a pleasant surprise on those rare occasions when reality exceeded both, as it did in this case. The cabin was charming! It was nestled among tall pines at the edge of a lake, with a view of the mountains beyond. Warm light glowed from the windows. There was no one in sight. No honking horns or loud voices assaulting the air, no sketchy characters lurking in shadows, and best of all, no bosses dropping work on her desk.

*Merry Christmas, Abbie.*

The key code the owner had sent her worked, which was always a good sign. She walked inside and looked about. It was as charming inside as outside. She couldn't believe it was real, let alone hers for a week. She walked past a floor-to-ceiling fieldstone fireplace with built-in bookshelves on either side, and on into the bedroom. Opposite the bed, flanked by two tall windows, was a bricked-off fireplace containing an array of pillar candles. She set down her bag and fished out a bottle of wine and a corkscrew and went back through the living room to the kitchen. It was fitted with quartz countertops, black stainless steel appliances, and mission-style cabinets, all of which balanced its original mountain character with modern convenience.

Abbie shook her head. "I'm never going home."

Beyond the kitchen was a second bedroom, which looked as if it had been added on later. Abbie imagined the couple who'd built it standing in the kitchen, for no reason except that was where Abbie happened to be at the moment. The husband would walk in and find the wife cooking. She'd stop and gaze into his eyes while her own eyes shone. She would tell him they were going to have a baby. Then they would embrace. Abbie's heart swelled with unexpected emotion. It was all so romantic.

And not real. Wait, what was that sound? Oh, just her biological clock going off again. She hit the figurative snooze button. Oh well, in lieu of romance, wine would do. She set about attending to this most pressing need. The kitchen was well supplied with dishes, cooking pots, and utensils, and with what mattered most at the moment, wine glasses.

"God, I love this place." She poured a glass half full —ever the optimist—and went to the living room, where she sank into an overstuffed chair by the fireplace. The room was so cozy—so perfect for Christmas.

That was when she began to feel cold. While she was up getting a blanket, she pulled her e-book reader from her bag in the bedroom then found the thermostat and adjusted the setting to warm the place up. After plopping back down on the comfy chair, she stretched her legs out on the ottoman and spread the throw blanket on top. With a contented sigh, she took another sip of cabernet as the wind picked up and howled outside. Come to think of it, she had heard something about a Nor'easter on the car radio. No problem. She was snuggled inside her cabin with a bottle of wine and enough food to last out any storm. With any luck, the storm would bring snow for Christmas tomorrow.

Abbie was happy.

By the time she had finished a chapter in the book she was reading, Abbie's nose and fingers were cold. She got up to adjust the thermostat again. There was no way it was seventy-two degrees in this place. She bent over to feel the heating vent. Nothing. The metal grate was as cold as she was.

When the temperature failed to improve minutes later, Abbie set down her phone, which was useless up here with no signal, and threw off her aptly named throw blanket. She'd noticed a phone in the kitchen, and she intended to see if it worked.

An hour later, Abbie picked up the phone for the fourth time—or was it the fifth? "Hello. Abbie Harper here. Again. It's still cold. Does it mean anything when your fingers turn black and slough off? I'm sure it's nothing. Am I rambling? It's the hypothermia talking. Look, are you getting my messages? You know... it would be really nice if you'd—oh, I don't know—call me back?" She slammed the phone down—a corded phone. Very *Little House on the Prairie*, she thought. I bet they were cold, too. But they always had a blazing fire in the fireplace.

She eyed the fireplace again. There were a couple of logs. She'd never lit a wood fire, but she'd seen a survival show once. If a guy could start a fire with a stick and a string, how hard could it be? She needed some kindling. If only she'd printed two copies of that legal brief. She supposed she could gather some twigs like a good pioneer woman. "Yeah, and then after that, I'll go plow the back forty," she mumbled as she put on her jacket.

She stepped outside and gasped. It was snowing! All the evergreen trees were dusted with snow, and the ground was all powdery white. It was perfect—except for the freezing. Now all she needed was heat. She found a few twigs and a couple of branches, which she broke—well, stomped—down to a size that would fit in the fireplace.

Back inside, she arranged everything in the fire-place a little too neatly. She fished a few crumpled receipts form her purse and slipped them between twigs and logs. Now to light them. Her efficiency at packing only went as far as bringing a corkscrew. A lighter had never made it to her computer-stored packing list. She made a mental note to correct that for the next trip. People laughed at her lists, but her world was a better place for them.

She made a fairly thorough search of the kitchen, which at last yielded a small, half-used box of wooden matches from one of the drawers. After a brief victory dance, she returned to the fireplace and, at last, lit the fire.

It was a glorious thing of warm beauty. And then the smoke began. It drifted into the room. Abbie opened the doors. It got worse. She couldn't breathe. Glancing about in a near panic, she spied the fire extinguisher and managed to figure out how it worked—she hoped. She aimed, leaned back, squinting, and sprayed. With that done, she opened the windows and cleared the cabin of smoke as well as any lingering heat.

This seemed like a good time to consider her options. Plan A: warm up in the car—but she'd driven on empty for the last several miles, there having been no gas station that stayed open after dusk in this remote wilderness. What little gas was left she would need to fuel her trip to the gas station in town for a refill. That killed plan B, which was to decamp and go home to spend Christmas with Taylor. By now, this far into Christmas Eve, there was a good chance nothing was open anywhere, so she didn't dare start for home. If she ran out of gas, she might wind up on the side of the road, with her subcompact rental car mauled by a bear. It was a perfectly logical causal relationship. So that left plan C, which was to stay here until her frozen body was found in the spring thaw. So she pulled all the covers off the bed and curled up on the sofa, where she finished her glass of wine and dozed off.

A loud clang woke her. Abbie sat bolt upright. The sound came from below. More clanging rang out. There was a door off the kitchen, which must lead to the cellar. She grimaced. Nothing good ever came from a single female going down to a cellar. She stood and glanced about for a weapon. After corking the wine bottle (waste not, want not), she grasped it and took a step forward. And stopped. She turned back for a fortifying sip of wine. Hmm... she might need another, so she brought the glass in one hand and her weapon, the bottle, in the other. A few stealthy steps later, the noise stopped. "Someone needs to go down there." She looked at her wine glass and whispered, "You go first."

She had to do something, but what? Go downstairs to investigate? Nope. Make a mad dash for the car? Maybe. And then maybe run out of gas before getting to safety. Or she could call the police and hide until they arrived. But the phone was across the room. If she went there, she'd be farther from the door—and her car.

No, she would go for the car. It was a commitment but might be the best thing to do. *Dammit.* The keys were in her purse in the bedroom. If she went there and he—or she—followed her, there'd be no way out except through a window. Did the windows even open? It was an old house. They might be painted shut. But there'd been a number of upgrades, and very well done, at that. *Focus, Abbie, focus!*

A door closed loudly downstairs. Abbie flinched. Footsteps resonated from the wraparound porch. She couldn't just stand here. She had to do something. She went to the front door and stood behind it, wine bottle at the ready. A loud knock on the door made her jump.

# THREE

"Ms. Harper?"

How did he know her name? *Abbie, is that really the key issue here?* What if some disgruntled legal opponent had a grudge against her and had followed her up here? Sure, she practiced corporate law, but maybe some evil corporation had hired a hit man to avoid a contentious arbitration. On the other hand, it could just be a serial burglar—or an evil huntsman!

"Are you all right?"

Why would an evil hit man/burglar/huntsman want to know that?

"Ms. Harper!" He rattled the door.

But why was he rattling the door when he'd been in the cellar, a mere flight of stairs and unlocked door away? Well, he was here now. Was this really the time to be pondering questions like that?

The door flew open. Abbie flinched and pulled back her wine bottle and swung at him, but a firm hand grasped her wrist before she could strike.

"Abbie Harper?" He held her wrist firmly.

"None of your business!"

"I'm Jack."

She looked at him, too stunned to speak. For an evil huntsman, he wasn't bad looking—not to mention polite. In such moments, most nefarious intruders might have dispensed with formalities like introductions, but not this one.

"Jack Whelan. The owner? Of this cabin?"

Her jaw dropped. She inhaled. "You're—"

The corner of his mouth turned up. He gently pried the wine bottle from her grasp and let go of her wrist. "I got your messages. All seven of them." He leveled a look that made her shiver—and not from the cold.

She balked. "No... seven? There couldn't have been more than five."

He stared into her eyes.

Feeling suddenly foolish, she said, "Well, maybe six. Look, I'm sorry. I was cold."

"Well, it should be warming up soon. I just came upstairs to check. Sorry to disturb you." He glanced at her wine bottle on his way to check each vent, finally pausing at the thermostat. He sniffed and went over to the fireplace. "What happened here?"

"Oh."

"That's not really an answer." He directed a pointed look that unsettled her.

She wished he'd stop doing that. She tried not to look guilty as the sight of the smoke-filled cabin came back to her. Instead, she managed to look defensive. "I was cold, so I tried to light a fire."

She did not appreciate the puzzled frown that came next. "I didn't burn the house down or anything. It just got a little too smoky, so I put it out."

He crouched down and looked at the fireplace. With a beckoning gesture, he said, "Come here."

She did. As if crouching down close by the cold fireplace with a hot guy didn't feel awkward enough— not to mention a little too close—he gave her a look that was subtle, but condescending, just the same.

"This is a flue. When you want a fire, open it so the smoke can go up through the chimney instead of into the room. When there's no fire, close it so the cold air doesn't come down through the chimney and—"

"Right. Got it." She looked away to hide her embarrassment.

He flipped the lever a couple of times.

"Now you try."

She did not even try to hide how much this annoyed her. "Thank you, I get how a lever works."

He smiled, even white teeth and all. "Judging by the smoky smell and the fire extinguisher residue, I'd say you needed a little refresher course."

He was lucky his smile had distracted her from her annoyance, or he'd have heard about it. Instead, she just lowered her eyes, mainly to escape that smile and how much she enjoyed it. She flipped the lever up and down a couple of times. "There, happy?"

Instead of answering her with a simple yes or no, which would have been the appropriate response, he lifted his chin toward the wine bottle. "Can I pour you another? You seem like you could use it."

"And what's that supposed to mean?"

He suppressed a smile but said nothing. Instead, he got up, offered his hand to help her do the same, and then topped up her glass. "Mind if I join you? If you couldn't use it, I could."

Abbie watched, slack-jawed, as he went to the kitchen and helped himself to a wine glass. She almost snarked, "Make yourself at home," but remembered he was at home. This was his cabin. But it was her personal space, which she'd rented for the week. She supposed she should feel more uncomfortable now than she actually did. But he'd mentioned in an email that he was a forest ranger, so that made him safe, right? Surely they vetted those guys pretty well. She studied him. He was a good six feet tall—a bad six being just plain tall without all the broad shoulders and muscly manliness. Yeah, he was a very good six feet tall. He returned from the kitchen, glass in hand, and set it down while he squatted down and built a fire. From where Abbie was sitting, she could not help but notice—well, yes, the view, and also—that he knew his way around a fireplace. But back to the view...

Jack settled into the sofa and took what could not in all honesty be called a sip. He was thirsty. He tossed an unexpectedly bashful look her way. "I'm sorry. I wasn't really thinking. I'm actually your guest, aren't I? And I've kind of made myself at home."

Abbie found herself shrugging. "No problem."

He offered his glass, and they toasted. "Merry Christmas!"

"Oh, I've got something for you! Wait here." He leapt up and went outside. He returned, stomped his feet on the door mat, and handed her a bottle of Champagne. "Here. For Christmas. Or you could save it for New Year's Eve."

"Thank you." This guy would not let her stay annoyed with him. She took it to the fridge and turned back to catch him tipping his wine glass and finishing it off.

He brought it to the kitchen and put it in the dishwasher. Abbie now was in a state of sheer wonder. He was neat. This could be the makings of a big, giant, uppercase LOVE.

He looked up and caught her grinning but had the good taste not to comment. "If you have any more trouble with the heat, well, I guess you know how to reach me."

She felt her cheeks flush as she lifted her eyes. *Oh great, the phone calls again. And I'm blushing. I've just time traveled back to middle school.* She dug down deep and managed a businesslike nod. As she walked him to the door, she had nearly recovered her equanimity when she looked outside. "Oh wow, look at the snow—and that truck! Oh my gosh, you're the jerk!" She looked up at him, outraged. "You practically T-boned me this morning!"

Well, that was a relief. She was starting to find this guy way too attractive. Which was weird, because longish brown hair, yesterday's stubble, plaid shirts, well-worn jeans, and work boots laced halfway up were not normally her thing. Not that she'd paid much attention. But he had a look, and he wore that look well —tall and strapping, with an intriguing air.

A pained look crossed his face. "That was you? I'm sorry."

"Yeah? Well, you should be. Do you always drive like that?"

His eyes softened. "No. My dog got into some Christmas chocolate someone sent me. I'd left the package on the table. It was a gift, so I hadn't opened it yet. I should've checked to make sure it was safe or put it up out of reach."

Abbie wasn't quite following. "I'm sorry. So he got into some chocolate. And that gives you permission to drive recklessly?"

He regarded her as if she were the fool. "Chocolate's toxic for dogs."

Abbie's brows lifted. "Oh. Well, I'm not really a dog person, so I had no idea. Wow...chocolate. Go figure." She shrugged. She might have been reading things into this, but she got the clear impression that she'd just lost his respect—not that she cared, but still.

He said, "I was afraid I might lose him, so I raced to the vet."

"I'm so sorry. How is he?"

He looked grateful for her having asked. "He's okay. The vet thinks he'll be fine. To be safe, she's keeping him overnight for observation."

Abbie nodded. "That must've been so scary."

"If he'd eaten much more, he'd have died. So, yeah, it was scary."

Abbie felt like a jerk. The poor guy had been valiantly saving his dog. Her stomach sank as she remembered her phone messages.

"I'm so sorry. And then I had to call you six times."

"Seven." His eyes lit with a hint of amusement.

"I'm so sorry." Abbie wondered if there were a statutory limit on how many times one could say that.

He shook his head to dismiss it as if it had been nothing. Or maybe he hoped it would prevent her from saying she was so sorry—again. He exhaled and stood. "It's all good. My dog's fine. And your heat's back on."

"Thank you." She felt a surge of pride for having managed to say something different—not unique or interesting, but still...

He glanced toward the door and then back at her. "Is there anything else that you need?"

Her inner self answered, *You.* But she smiled and said, "No."

"Good." He gave a nod toward the fireplace. "Remember the flue."

She nodded. "Got it." She caught herself nodding like a life-sized bobblehead, so she stopped and smiled again. Talk about needlessly awkward. But that was her gift. Would her middle school self ever leave her grown-up body?

His brow creased. "Are you going to be okay here alone?"

"I live alone every day in the big city, so I guess I can manage it here." As soon as she'd said it, she knew that she sounded defensive, not to mention the fact that her logic was way off the mark.

He looked into her eyes. "Yeah, I'm sorry. I just thought. Well, it's Christmas."

Her heart skipped a beat. She looked toward the door to hide her reaction. A warmth had come through his eyes and his words that had touched her. Color came into her cheeks. She pulled it together and looked straight into his eyes—they were gray. "Thank you. I'm fine. I just needed some time to myself."

As if he could possibly understand how she felt without pitying her, he looked at her with a warmth that took her off guard. "Then I'll leave you to it."

His manner changed. With a Ranger Jack nod, he went to the door. "Merry Christmas, Ms. Harper."

"Abbie."

He repeated her name. For some reason, it sounded like Christmas magic—as if an angel got his wings when he said her name.

"Merry Christmas, Mr.—"

"Jack," he corrected her, grinning.

"Jack."

She watched through the storm door as he drove his old pickup down the driveway through the six inches of snow that continued to fall.

"Jack Whelan."

# FOUR

ABBIE TURNED on the outdoor lights and pulled open all of the curtains so she could see the snow fall from wherever she was in the cabin. Big, fluffy flakes fell and had already covered the ground and the tips of the balsam fir branches. From time to time, wind would toss it about like a scene in a snow globe. The TV weather reporter chattered away in the background. The Nor'easter had shifted and was now tracking toward the Adirondacks, changing snowfall projections to as much as two feet.

No worries. Abbie had food—all the Christmas trimmings and holiday beverages and treats enough for a week of cabin-bound bliss. If there was one thing Abbie could do, it was plan. She had ordered a take-away Christmas dinner from Stew Leonard's in Yonkers and had left home early enough to pick it up before it had become too insanely packed with last-minute food shoppers. The only thing she was missing was a tree.

Tromping through the fresh snow in back, Abbie came to a stop a few yards into the woods and looked about. Spying just the thing, she broke off an evergreen branch and brought it inside. She cut the end off with a kitchen knife then put the small branch in a water-filled canning jar. She stood back and admired it with a grin. Now she had a Christmas tree.

The sound of spinning tires drew her to the window. Jack's truck was back, fishtailing its way up the driveway. He came to a stop behind her car, now a smooth white curve with no visible tires. The wind had picked up, blowing snow until Jack nearly disappeared in the white haze. She called out to him, and he came back into view. When he reached the front porch, he stomped the snow off his boots and brushed it off his clothes.

Before Abbie could ask, he said, "A tree fell and took out the small bridge down the road. There's no way out." He left his boots on the boot tray and went to the kitchen, where he hung his coat, hat, and gloves on hooks by the back door. The clinging snow was beginning to melt.

Abbie stared. "No way out...at all?"

"Not until the storm blows over." He went to the

fire and warmed his hands, then he took off his socks and draped them over the screen.

Abbie wrinkled her nose as she looked at the socks. "But there must be a way. You're a ranger."

He pulled a chair closer to the fire and stretched out his long legs. "Yeah, they're going to be down one man until tomorrow." He abruptly got up and went to the kitchen and stuck his head into the fridge. "Have you got any beer?"

"No. And what about snowmobiles?"

"To drink?"

She rolled her eyes. "No, to drive."

"First of all, I don't have one."

"But somebody else could come get you."

He shook his head. "I could barely see the house on my way from the truck. I can't ask someone to risk their life coming out in white-out conditions when I'm safe and warm here."

"So I guess snowshoes are out of the question." Abbie glanced at the antique wooden pair hanging over the fireplace. Then she caught sight of the smirk on Jack's face and averted her eyes. Even she knew it was a ridiculous notion to send him out in blizzard conditions on those rickety things. With a defeated sigh, she went to the kitchen. "There's no beer. Will wine do?"

As he followed and watched her pour him a glass of wine, he said, "If it makes you feel any better, when

I was down at the bridge, I had pretty much the same conversation over the radio—well, minus the snowshoes."

The corner of his mouth turned up just enough to make Abbie sure he was laughing at her—on the inside, at least. He grew suddenly serious. "I'm sorry. I know this wasn't the Christmas you had in mind."

Abbie looked at him frankly. "What about you? I'm sure you had plans."

They went back to the living room and sat on the sofa facing the fireplace. Jack said, "The usual—Christmas with family."

Abbie felt a twinge of disappointment then guilt. "Mrs. Ranger Jack isn't going to like it—not to mention the mini rangers."

"There's no Mrs. Ranger Jack or any mini rangers —just my parents, my brother, his wife, and their mini Whelan on the way." He smiled and looked into her eyes.

She wished he'd stop doing that, because those gray eyes made her heart skip a beat. That she could take, but she'd read that pupils dilated when you were attracted to someone. A few more of those looks, and her eyes would be horror-film black.

She said, "Small family."

He nodded. "It's all I've ever known, so it's normal for me. How about you?"

Her smirk spread to a smile. "Smaller."

"Do they live far away?" He looked puzzled.

"No, not very."

"Then why...? I'm sorry, that's none of my business."

Abbie took a moment to think about how much she wanted to share with this guy she'd just met. "My mother and stepfather went on a cruise. They asked me to join them, but I was afraid Santa wouldn't find us so far out at sea, so I declined."

He studied her, which made her feel that she had to explain. "I wanted cold weather and snow for my Christmas." She glanced at the window, where snow was piling up on the sill. "Careful what you wish for! And I needed a break from, well, people."

"People or a person?" He pivoted on the sofa to face her, chin in hand.

She shook her head. "No, there's no person. I work too much to interact with humans."

"But you must work with humans. You're a lawyer, aren't you?"

"I think calling them human is a stretch."

"What kind of law?"

"Corporate." Abbie's voice softened. "There's a lot of stress in my work, so I thought this would be a nice place to have the sort of Christmas I've always wanted."

"But never had?"

"I didn't say that."

"But you meant it."

"Am I on a witness stand?" Her annoyed look drew a smile.

He leaned back, smile fading except in his eyes. He was studying her, and she knew it. She glanced away and gazed at the fire.

After a few moments of quiet, he said, "So what is the perfect Christmas for Abbie Harper, Esquire?"

Without taking her eyes from the fire, she said, "Not much, really. A fire, maybe candles, and another glass of wine..." She leaned forward, but he sprang up and went to the kitchen.

He returned moments later with the wine bottle in hand. "Fewer trips this way."

That smile of his was something. Even, white teeth. Full lips. "Abbie?"

She glanced up with a start but recovered as she took her refilled glass from him. Their hands brushed and set off an inner alarm. "Candles. Hold on." She went into the bedroom and returned with a half dozen votive candles and holders.

Jack held out his hand, and she gave him a few.

"Where would you like them?"

Abbie looked about. "I guess across the mantel."

While she adjusted their final placement, Jack lit

the candles. He glanced at the table across the room. "Is that your Christmas tree?"

Abbie ignored his obvious amusement. "Yes."

"Where did you get it?"

"Out back."

"You know, back in the day, they used to arrest people for stealing Christmas trees from park land."

"That's park land back there?"

He nodded. "Actually, they just issued tickets to first-time offenders."

"Go on, then. Write me up."

"I don't think anyone's written a ticket for that in some time."

"Why? Are you guys slacking off?"

"No." He sounded a little defensive. "I think people around here finally got that it's not such a good thing to do."

She looked at her Christmas branch with a frown. "This isn't a tree. It's a branch. So I'm innocent."

"Maybe." He sighed. "Okay, I'll let you off with a warning."

With a wry look, she said, "Wow, it's my lucky day, isn't it?"

He shrugged in tacit agreement then turned his attention to the branch. "It's not much of a Christmas tree without decorations. Got any?"

"When I was a girl, we used to make cookie ornaments."

"Well, come on, then." Without waiting for her, Jack went straight to the kitchen and looked through the cupboards.

"I'm a step ahead of you, Jack." She pulled a roll of cookie dough out of the fridge.

When he saw it, Jack grinned like a ten-year-old kid. "Now what do we need?"

Abbie called out items while Jack found them. She said, "A rolling pin? This is a well-equipped kitchen for a rental."

"It was my grandparents' cabin. I left a lot of their stuff in the cupboards."

He had such a wistful look on his face as he looked at the cabinets that Abbie hesitated before interrupting. Rolling pin in hand, she said, "Ready?"

They laughed their way through the rolling and cutting. When they pulled the cookies out of the oven, they shared the same perplexed expression. Instead of the flat sugar cookies they were expecting, their tray was filled with fluffy creatures that bore no resemblance to what they'd cut out minutes ago.

Jack shook his head. "That reindeer looks like something that leapt out of the black lagoon."

Abbie couldn't take her eyes from the tray. "Our gingerbread men have beer guts."

"It happens."

"It shouldn't."

He put his hands on her shoulders and guided her out of the kitchen. "Go sit down and pretend this never happened."

"But we have to take them off of the cookie sheet."

"I'll do it. Why don't you find us some music."

A few minutes later, carols were quietly playing from Abbie's Bluetooth speaker. Abbie returned to the kitchen to find Jack sneaking a cookie. "Hungry?"

Mouth full, he helplessly nodded.

She pulled out a loaf of hearth-baked bread, almost homemade soup, and sliced meats and cheeses. They each made their own sandwich and sat down at the table, with the Christmas branch in the center.

Between bites, Abbie asked, "What's your favorite Christmas Eve tradition?"

"The usual, I guess."

Abbie's brow furrowed. "Such as...?"

"Oh, you know. My brother and I would watch Christmas movies."

"Me, too." An image of her childhood came to mind.

Jack watched her. "Not happy?"

"No, I'm fine."

"I meant your Christmases. As a child. They weren't happy?"

She looked frankly at him. "Not always."

He was quiet for a long while. "One of our traditions was to help our drunk father to bed. When my brother and I were too young to carry him, we'd leave him on the floor with a pillow and blanket." He chuckled. "I used to worry that Santa would trip over him." Jack looked down for a moment. "He's sober now—has been for years." A smile came and went quickly.

Abbie looked off toward the fire as "Count Your Blessings (Instead of Sheep)" played. "No advanced math skills needed in my house for that one." She forced a weak smile. "My parents did their fighting upstairs in their bedroom, but I could still hear them. I'd watch Christmas movies to drown out the noise. I saved *White Christmas* for last. I don't know why it was my favorite. I was just a child." Abbie got up and took her plate to the kitchen. The cabin had an open layout, but a small portion of the kitchen was concealed from the great-room table. Abbie went there and took a few deep breaths. She was wiping her eyes just as Jack walked in with his plate.

He said softly, "We're not those kids anymore. We don't have to feel like that now."

"No, but holidays have a way of dredging up old feelings." She blotted her eyes on the dish towel. "I'm not like this. It's just... I get this way at Christmas sometimes."

"Abbie." He bent down and tried to make eye contact. When she wouldn't look at him, he lifted her chin. "It's okay."

She looked into his eyes and started to shake her head, but he opened his arms, and she went to him as if she belonged there. She softly exhaled. It was as though she'd come home. He was warm and gentle, and he smelled good—not cologne, maybe soap. She breathed in and sank into his strong chest and enfolding arms, with her head resting under his chin. It felt good.

And that was her cue to step back. She hadn't thought that one through. Her face brightened. "Well, right on schedule. Christmas Eve meltdown? Check. Let's see, what's next on the list? Ah yes, dishes and Christmas tree decorating." She didn't look at him to see how he reacted. She didn't want to know. Either he thought she was crazy, which would show he was a good judge of character; or he was looking all soft-hearted and sympathetic, which would just make her melt into an uglier mess; or the physical contact had engaged his man hormones, and comfort had transmuted into lust. He was a guy. It was what they did. She had hormones, too, but her feelings overrode them. She couldn't help it. She couldn't do anything casually. Curse of the obsessive-compulsive over-achiever.

Well, that was the fastest she'd ever done dishes. She dried off her hands as if she were Lady Macbeth.

Jack gently took the towel from her and hung it over the oven handle. "Let's go decorate the tree."

And that was that. He didn't question her behavior or find her display of emotion alarming or distasteful. He didn't analyze her feelings in an effort to fix her, or try to convince her that they made no sense. That was weird and refreshing. The hug, however, had been a mistake. Even so, he hadn't tried to force something from it that was never intended. That would have caused complications. Even if there were genuine feelings, they had nowhere to go. There was never going to be an "Abbie & Jack" or even "Abbie's One-Night Stand." She had a bad habit of caring, and that led to hurting. She just didn't want to. That meant she didn't have to. Once she'd figured that out, her life had become so much simpler.

Jack sat down and fiddled with a yarn needle and ribbon until he noticed her watching. He gave up and helplessly handed them to her. "These clumsy hands can't seem to get the job done."

Abbie barely refrained from raising an eyebrow. She imagined that was one of the few jobs those hands couldn't get done—and well. He had large, manly hands, the kind Taylor called "man paws." Abbie tore her gaze away from his hands and focused on threading the needle. That done, they looped ribbons through the cookies and hung their misshapen creations on the Christmas branch.

"We'd better stop now before they tip over our tree."

Abbie nodded, and they put the leftovers away. On their way back, they paused at the table and stood side by side to examine their finished creation.

Abbie shook her head. "Hideous."

Jack nodded. "Yup."

And they both walked away.

## FIVE

JACK GAZED THROUGH THE WINDOW. Snow continued to fall in large, fluffy flakes that weighed down the tree limbs and covered the ground in a smooth blanket of white. Abbie's car was nearly hidden by snow, and beside it was a white mound vaguely shaped like a truck. It felt as though they were alone in the world, safe and warm, in a place where nothing mattered except the two of them as they discovered each other. He had an uncanny sense that it was all meant to be.

He shook off the feeling and turned to find Abbie studying the contents of the bookcase near the fireplace. She smiled, pulled out a book, and sat down on the sofa to thumb through it. At some point, while he wasn't looking, she'd put on some glasses. Strands of nut-brown hair had slipped free of the doubled-over knot at the nape of her neck. He had an impulse to reach out and run his fingers along that long neck, but somehow he resisted.

He almost hated to disturb her, she was so lost in that book. But he sat down beside her and leaned over to see what she was reading. "Yeats. My grandmother loved her Irish poets. They reminded her of home."

"She was Irish, then?"

"No." He shrugged and then laughed when her eyes narrowed with confusion. "Sorry. Just amusing myself. Cabin fever. Yeah, she was Irish—and my grandfather, too." He held out his hand. "May I?" She put the book in his hand, and he read aloud.

> When you are old and grey and full
>     of sleep,
> And nodding by the fire, take down
>     this book,
> And slowly read, and dream of the
>     soft look
> Your eyes had once, and of their
>     shadows deep;
>
> How many loved your moments of
>     glad grace,

And loved your beauty with love false
    or true,
But one man loved the pilgrim soul
    in you,
And loved the sorrows of your
    changing face;

And bending down beside the glowing
    bars,
Murmur, a little sadly, how Love fled
And paced upon the mountains
    overhead
And hid his face amid a crowd of stars.

He finished and looked up at Abbie. She stared at the fire, looking so far away. Jack wished he could join her. "My grandfather gave this book to my grandmother. My grandmother once said it was romantic. Looking back, I think he might have read it to her hoping to get lucky. But you can't deny the poem's romantic."

Abbie's brow wrinkled. "I think it's sad, really."

That wasn't quite the reaction he was expecting.

"But he loved her." Jack found himself wondering what it would be like to love someone like that. He had cared about a few women and thought that it might grow to love, but he'd never felt like this poet—or as his grandfather had for his grandmother. He sometimes wondered if he ever would.

Abbie said, in her smooth, quiet voice, "And she didn't love him. Underneath all of his beautiful words, he was saying that one day she'd be sorry. No one would love her like he did. But by the time she realized it, it would be too late."

Jack shook his head slowly, a glint in his eyes. "Women."

Abbie laughed. "You can't live with 'em—"

Jack joined in. "And you can't live without 'em."

Abbie got up and put the poetry book back on the shelf. "It's Christmas Eve. Let's be happy."

Jack pointed at Abbie's phone. "Let's see what's on that playlist."

She unlocked it and handed it to him. After scrolling a bit and offering a few nods of approval interspersed with disapproving glances her way, he found a classic holiday song. He sprang up and held out his hand. When she hesitated, he said, "C'mon. Don't tell me you don't dance."

"Oh, I dance. Just not well." She smiled and took hold of his hand. Jack swept her into his arms, and they danced. At first, it was unexpectedly awkward. Her body was so close to his. She averted her eyes, convincing him that she felt it, too. Jack recovered and lightened the mood by twirling her and then dipping her back.

Abbie laughed. "Don't drop me!"

He took this as an invitation to dip her back further while he bent over and held her suspended.

"Jack." Her face looked taut.

He looked into her eyes with a devilish glee. "Yes?"

"Let me go."

He loosened his grip just enough to make her gasp and clutch his arms.

Her face blanched. "Let me up."

He immediately did. "Abbie, I'm sorry. I was just having some fun."

"Being suspended upside down with no control over whether I fall on the floor is not my idea of fun." She avoided his eyes.

Jack was surprised by the strength of her reaction. "So I guess a Christmas bungee jump would be out of the question."

She leveled a look that made him pity her legal opponents—and now himself. "Sorry, Abbie. I had no idea."

"No idea of what?" She lifted her chin, practically scowling.

"That it would make you so uncomfortable. I guess I'm an unfeeling jerk."

"No, you're not! It's me. I'm just not much of a daredevil."

Jack couldn't help staring. "Uh... rappelling down a vertical rock face is daring. Being held in my arms—and, by the way, I work out—is pretty safe."

She looked doubtful.

"I wouldn't hurt you."

Sooner or later, a moment came in every relationship where the wheels began to spin off. Not that this was a relationship, exactly. It was more of a situation that had forced them together. He had barged in on her Christmas—through no fault or choice of his own. Still, he was here, and there was something between them. When had that happened? At what point had they kicked it up several notches to relationship status? He took a deep breath and exhaled. *Get a grip.*

Abbie's sweet voice interrupted his thoughts. "You're right. I overreacted."

His eyes softened. "No, you reacted. And now I will know to be gentle with you."

She looked into his eyes, and he thought—hoped—she would look up at him as if she wanted a kiss. There was always a look in the moment before.

"Have you ever rappelled down a vertical rock face?"

But this wasn't that look or that moment. "Yes." *And it wasn't as scary as this.*

With a slight nod, she said, "Yeah, you seem like the type who can't get enough outdoorsy danger."

"It's not so dangerous if you know what you're doing." *Wish I knew what I was doing right now.* It was his turn to feel out of control.

Abbie said, "I guess you must feel pretty confident out there."

"Well, yeah. It's my job—part of it."

"Oh. I hadn't really thought about it. I thought you just—I don't know—checked people into campsites and watched out for forest fires."

"And fight them. A big part of my job is saving people—sometimes from themselves. They go out for fun and get lost or stuck. Someone has to go help them. That's me—and the other rangers I work with."

"And you just risk your life for strangers, no big deal."

"People's lives are a big deal."

Abbie's eyes had a soft look of admiration he didn't deserve. But he couldn't look away, and he wanted to kiss her. They drew close. His lips parted, then hers.

"How 'bout some eggnog?" Abbie escaped to the kitchen.

"Uh—yeah. Sure." *What was that?* He could use a drink, too, preferably something with liquor. For some reason, he could hear Mason saying, "Liquor? I barely know her!" for the sixty-seventh time. The guy loved a good joke—again and again.

Jack dragged his fingers through his hair. He was mentally rambling, a sure sign he was nervous. Abbie did this to him. He reflected on that for a moment.

She returned with two glasses of eggnog, well spiked, he was pleased to discover. He thanked her and cheerily said, "What we need is a Christmas movie." *To distract me from wanting to climb all over your side of the sofa.*

Her face lit up. "I've brought my favorites." She went to the bedroom and returned with a stack of movies, which they went through one by one.

"Not in the mood." Abbie tossed it aside.

"Too girly." Jack handed it back.

Making note, Abbie thumbed through the next six and sent them straight to the reject pile.

He grabbed one of them. "Oh, I forgot about him." When she started to pull it from the rejects, he shook his head.

Jack lifted his eyebrows as she picked up another. "Maybe." Abbie set it aside and picked up the next one.

"That's a Christmas movie?" Jack frowned and tilted his head.

With a defensive tone, Abbie said, "Technically."

Jack shrugged. "Okay."

Having finally agreed on one, they got perfectly cozy on opposite ends of the sofa, sharing a blanket. As the opening credits rolled, Abbie grinned and said, "This is perfect."

Hearing that made Jack happier than it should have. Outside, the snow fell, and the wind howled, but inside, the flickering light from the fireplace reflected on the ceiling and walls. A Christmas movie was playing, and Abbie was practically glowing, blanket clutched contentedly to her chest. Christmas Eve. She was right. It was perfect.

Then the power went out.

Abbie said, "Maybe it'll come back on."

"Maybe." Having gone through this a few times every year, he knew better. He looked at Abbie, who was staring at the fire. Between that and the candles, they had enough light. "It's going to get cold. We'll need more blankets." He went through the house and brought back all he could find. With that done, he looked at Abbie. "Tired?"

"Tired, yes. Sleepy, no."

A burning log fell apart and sent sparks up the chimney. Abbie said, "Aside from the power issues, this is such a great cabin. Why don't you live here?"

Jack said, "I will eventually. When my grandparents died, no one else wanted it, really. It needed some work. My family all live around here, and they had their own homes. I did, too. Well, a rental in town. So, there we all were with equal shares of this cabin that no one else wanted, so I cashed in my savings and bought them all out. I don't really know why."

Abbie gazed into his eyes. "Because you love it here."

"I do."

"I can see why."

Jack looked around. "My grandparents put so much of themselves into this place. It was hard for them, in the end, to maintain it. And then my grandfather died, and my grandmother was gone a month later."

Abbie said, "That happens sometimes."

Jack nodded. "With people truly in love, so I've heard. Anyway, it wasn't in the best shape, so I've been working on it in my spare time. But I ran out of money."

"So you rent it out—"

"For the income. It covers the cost of the repair and renovation." He finished her thought.

"Well, I love it. Everything that you've done is just... right."

Jack was pleased. "It's getting there. I've got a few more things on my to-do list. A new furnace, for instance."

Abbie smirked, then her face lit up with a thought. "Oh, you know what would be great?"

His eyes narrowed with reserved curiosity. "What?"

"A generator."

Jack laughed. "Look at you with your crazy ideas."

"I know," she said, grinning.

"But, Miss Know-It-All, if we had power, we probably wouldn't be having this talk. Look how many fun facts you've pried out of me."

"True."

"And now it's your turn." Jack shifted his position, drawing closer to face her directly. "Why are you here, exactly?"

Awkward silence prevailed until Abbie's eyes lit up. "Two-bedroom, one-bath waterfront cabin with two wood-burning fireplaces, fully equipped kitchen, lake view, and short walk to... trees. It's all waiting for you at The Cabin."

"Oh, that ad. Not only can't I read poetry, I can't write it, either."

"It got my attention. Well, that, and it was available at the last minute, too."

"Yeah, too remote for some people."

"The wimps." Abbie rolled her eyes as she waved her hand dismissively. "What's a little road closure?"

Jack searched her eyes. "So what were you escaping from?"

Abbie shrugged, but Jack would not be distracted. "A guy?"

With a grimace, she said, "Why is it where a woman's concerned, people always assume it's a man? Maybe I've got other things going on in my life."

"Such as?"

"A job!"

"And?"

"You know... stuff."

"Stuff?"

Abbie avoided his gaze. "Yeah, so much stuff."

Her eyes narrowed. "And what's been going on in your life, Jack?" She appeared to enjoy sending the ball back to his court.

His mouth turned up a bit as he echoed her words. "Oh, you know, work stuff, cabin stuff, so much stuff."

In an instant, her lawyer face was back. "And women?"

His eyes glimmered with amusement. "I like them."

"In your personal life?"

"Yes."

Abbie's face lost its expression, but the wheels were turning. Was she disappointed? The thought pleased him.

He added, "But there's no one, at the moment."

Jack was way too happy to see her relief. "Or maybe there is someone... at the moment... Abbie..." He leaned closer.

ABBIE'S HEART POUNDED. Her lips parted. She turned abruptly away. "To answer your question, you were right. I'm here to escape. Yes, it's work, but it's also that everyone's life seems to complicate mine, which would not be so bad if a single person yielded any benefit from it. But they don't, including me. It's all just noise. And I needed to get away for some quiet, uncomplicated me time. No issues to deal with. No emotions... No men..."

Boom! Shot down! She could see it on his face, and she hadn't meant it to come across as sharply as it had.

Jack nodded. "This is a great place for that." He forced a smile. "Except for the part with, uh, me. I get it. I'm the last thing you wanted or needed."

She shook her head. "No, that's not what I meant —not in that way." The truth was, she was scared. Everything with Jack was electric—except for his house, at the moment. She'd just met him, and now it was as if her emotions had exploded all over the place and she needed to gather them up and contain them.

She needed time to think about this and to regain control.

With a kind smile, Jack said, "Let's get some sleep. In the morning, the weather will clear. With luck, the road will be plowed, and I'll be able to leave you to your quiet, uncomplicated week."

"Jack, I like you." Abbie quietly exhaled. There, she'd said it.

"I like you, too, Abbie. Good night." He got up, arranged his blankets, and lay down on the floor to sleep.

Abbie stretched out on the couch, pulled the covers up to her neck, and then counted the ways she hated herself until she fell asleep.

## SIX

JACK WOKE in the night and continued where he'd left off before falling asleep, chiding himself for having broken his own rule. If ever a woman had sent out signals to leave her alone, it was Abbie. But he had ignored every one. He couldn't blame her. In fact, he understood her point of view better than his own. What bothered him most was the fact that he cared. There was something between them—chemistry... or a magnetic pull, for lack of a better description—that he hadn't felt in a very long time, if ever. He had enjoyed his share of relationships, but the ones that had lasted for any length of time were the ones that were light, with a lot of emotional space between them. They'd go out, have some fun, and sometimes more. But there had always been an understanding of just what it was... and was not. This thing with Abbie was something he'd never felt before. He didn't blame her for bolting. It scared him, too.

Abbie cried out then sat up. Outside, coyotes were howling. "Oh, crap. I was hoping it was only a nightmare." She got up and went to the door.

"Abbie, what're you doing?"

Her voice sounded shaky. "Checking the locks." She proceeded to check the back door and the basement, along with the windows.

Jack met her as she emerged from the bedroom, grasping her shoulders to stop her. "What is it?"

Coyotes howled again, and she flinched.

"What, that?"

"Yes!" she said, as though it should be obvious.

He spoke calmly. "They won't hurt you. They're probably more afraid of you than you are of them."

"Oh, I doubt that." She glanced about. "Are you sure they can't get in?"

"Yes, I promise. Wow, you *are* a city girl. Look, it's okay. We're in the woods. There are going to be animals out there, but chances are, they'll leave us alone."

Alarm burned in her eyes. "Chances? I don't even buy lottery tickets! And you think that'll make me feel better?"

"Abbie, what is it?" Something was seriously

wrong, but it didn't make sense. She was inside, safe from anything out there that could harm her.

"Do you have to know everything about me?"

He let go, palms held helplessly upward. "Everything? It seems to me I've told you everything about me. I know nothing about you—which is fine." God knows, he didn't want to get shot down again. He got it. Back off. "I just need to know what's wrong so I can help you. Occupational hazard. I have to help people."

"Cynophobia."

He wrinkled his brow. "Fear of... signs?"

"Dogs."

"Dogs?" He tried to hide his disbelief.

"And wolves."

He nodded toward the window. "Those are coyotes."

"And coyotes. Also dingoes, I've read, though I've never actually seen one."

"So a trip to Australia is out of the question."

"The whole dog family, more or less, terrifies me." She nodded nervously. "Since I was a child. It's not such a problem in the city. I went to a therapist for it. Now I'm okay around dogs on leashes. I mean, I'm still nervous, but I can walk the long way around them on a sidewalk without embarrassing myself. It helps to live in a building where no pets are allowed." More howling sounded from outside. Abbie cast anxious eyes toward the window.

Jack was puzzled. "You must have known there would be animals up here in the heavily forested mountains."

"Well, bears, yes. But I did an Internet search, and it said that wolves were basically extinct in this area. I didn't think to look up coyotes. I thought they were only in old westerns."

"Wait, bears don't scare you?"

"Well, I'm not going to walk up to one and pet it, but no. Bears are different."

Jack shook his head. This time the howling was closer.

Abbie went to the kitchen and poured a healthy serving of cognac with a splash of eggnog and drank it.

"Down the hatch, then." Jack watched her, still trying to wrap his head around this new facet of the intriguing Abbie Harper.

When she lifted the bottle to pour another, Jack put his hand on hers and lowered the bottle. "Come here. I promise I won't try to kiss you."

She looked with teary eyes and sank into his open arms. Jack held her and soothed her until she was calm enough to go back to the sofa. They put on some music to distract from the noises outside, and Jack sat beside her, his arm about her shoulders. The howling continued intermittently in the hours that followed, but Jack was there with her.

Sunlight shone in through the cracks in the curtains. A loud knock awoke them as they lay sprawled together on the sofa. Jack sprang up and went to the door. His Siberian husky rushed in to greet him. Jack crouched down to greet him with a laugh. "Hey, Boomer. You missed me?" He looked up, still smiling. "Hi, Mason."

"Merry Christmas!" said Mason, a wiry guy with stringy light-brown hair, an easy smile, and a laid-back manner. The latter, along with his love of bad jokes, caused some to not take him seriously, but he had been there for Jack and was fearless under pressure. Mason looked across the room at Abbie, who watched the man's-best-friend reunion with fear in her eyes. In a low voice, he said, "Is she okay?"

Jack said, "Fear of dogs."

"You're kidding."

"Does anything here look funny?"

"Just you." Mason laughed.

Jack humored him with a smile. "Would you do me a favor and take Boomer to my truck?"

"Oh, you're not driving out of here. I just came to take you to your house for Christmas."

Jack looked past him to the snowmobile with an enclosed sled hitched to it.

Mason said, "I brought Boomer in the trailer, but your friend there—"

"Mason, this is Abbie."

Mason smiled, while Abbie forced a smile and a polite greeting through her nerves.

Mason continued, "I guess she could ride up front with me while you ride in the trailer with Boomer. I'm not sure if you'll fit there together, but it's worth a try."

"Oh, no thanks. You guys run along," Abbie said with a confident smile.

Mason said, "But the road is still closed. You'll be stranded."

"I know. I like it that way. Besides, the lights are back on. I'll be fine."

"Are you sure?"

Abbie nodded.

Jack tore his gaze away and turned to Mason. "Okay. I guess she'll stay here. Would you take Boomer outside? I'll be out in a minute."

Mason gave him a knowing smirk. "Sure, Jack. No problem."

Jack bent down to Boomer and gave him a pat, then he watched Mason lead Boomer toward the snowmobile before closing the door. He crossed the room and went to her. She was still trembling from meeting Boomer. "Will you be okay?"

"Sure."

She was not a good liar.

"I doubt you'll see or hear from the coyotes today. They're usually nocturnal."

"Usually?"

"On rare occasions, they might hunt for food in the daylight, but—look, if it makes you feel better, just stay inside until I get back."

"Get back?"

"I'm going home for Christmas dinner with my family, but after dinner, I can borrow a snowmobile and head back up here."

"No. I can't ask you to do that."

"You didn't. I offered. See you later." He gave her a hug and wished her a Merry Christmas. She didn't bristle, so that was encouraging.

ABBIE LOCKED THE FRONT DOOR, just in case a coyote with opposable thumbs managed to get past the latch, then she heaved a sigh. "Merry Christmas, Abbie." She still felt his arms about her as he hugged her good-bye.

An hour later, the living room was cleared of sleep-over bedding and she was enjoying a Gruyère cheese omelet and freshly ground pour-over coffee. The cabin was warm. The fireplace embers were glowing, and carols were playing. The start might have been rocky, but this was it—her perfect Christmas morning.

Her mind strayed to Jack. She wondered what he was doing right now. He was probably with his parents, brother, and sister-in-law. She wondered if his brother looked at all like him, with that tousled dark hair and those soft gray eyes. "Easy, girl." Jack was inside her head, and that wasn't good. "Time for a distraction. Let's open some presents. And then afterwards, maybe, stop talking to yourself."

She had a card-sized envelope from her mother and Doug, a large gift bag from Taylor, and a box she'd ordered for herself. She opened that first. It contained a pair of earrings that would look good with her navy suits. Taylor's gift bag was filled with soaps and toiletries from their favorite smelly soap shop. (It had a more elegant name.)

Abbie picked up the card from her mother and Doug, took a breath, and then tore off the edge and pulled out the card. She opened the glittery Christmas snow scene to a few lines of verse that she skimmed and forgot about the next moment. Taped on the left was a printout of an Internet gift card from... SoSoSingle.com? Plastered across the card was the slogan, "Find your so-so-someone!" She had overachieved her way through school, passed the bar, gotten a job as a lawyer in New York City, and her mother's takeaway from all that was that she needed a man. Great.

Then her mind wandered to Jack. *Argh!* She went to the sofa to read and caught sight of the poetry book. "If I read any more Yeats, I'll be hopeless." Instead, she put *White Christmas* on the TV. Soon, the previous night's lack of sleep caught up with her, and she dozed off.

When she awoke, the credits were rolling. She went to the window and looked out at the snow. She was restless, but the snow was too deep to walk through—or run through while fleeing from a pack of rabid coyotes. Never mind. Even if the whole driveway were plowed to the main road, she would not step one foot outside alone knowing they were out there. So she gathered her soaps and bath salts and indulged in a hot bubble bath complete with a flute of Champagne.

She topped off the leisurely bath with a cozy Christmas novella, followed by a candlelit dinner for one. It was as peaceful as she'd ever wished a Christmas to be. She promised herself that if she ever had children (leaving out the part about who would father them), she'd make sure every Christmas was as perfect for them as this was for her.

Her phone reached the end of the playlist, and the cabin was quiet. No coyotes... no Jack. That was her cue to get up and busy herself. There were dishes to do, although not very many from a warmed-up takeout dinner. After pouring a post-dinner eggnog, she went to sit down and enjoy it. It was quiet, no email to answer, no phone calls, no meetings to get to. Sheer bliss.

So why was she finding it so hard to be here all alone? She lived alone in the city. She worked long hours, and when she was home, she spent half her time there working, too. Work consumed nearly all of her days. Or she let it. Was that all her life was or was going to be? Maybe it was time to take stock.

## SEVEN

JACK PARKED the snowmobile and knocked on the cabin door. When she opened the door, the warm light from inside the cabin was nothing to the light from her eyes.

"Merry Christmas!" He gave her a quick hug and walked in. They exchanged warm smiles and small talk about their days being fine, and then there was awkward silence.

"The candles look nice." More smiles.

She said, "I lit a fire—flue open this time."

"Good for you." Jack grinned. "You look nice." If "nice" meant "hot and I want to hold you against me."

Her brow furrowed. "It's just jeans and a sweater."

"I know." Jack inwardly groaned. At the rate he was going, he'd be monosyllabic before he'd finished stepping out of his boots. He hung his jacket on one of the hooks by the door and turned back to face Abbie. The cabin looked better with her in it. Even the Christmas branch looked good, which was his first clue he was falling for her. He was no longer thinking rationally.

"Well, come in, sit down. It feels weird inviting you into your own place."

"But it's yours for the week." He looked down at the six-pack of local craft beer he was holding. "Oh, I brought these. Would you like me to put them in the fridge?"

"No, you sit down. Would you like one?"

"I would."

"I'll be right back."

Abbie went to the kitchen and stopped as soon as she was out of view. She was breathless, heart pounding. She took a few deep, silent breaths, checked her pulse, and then took her time pouring the drinks while she calmed herself down. A few minutes later, she emerged, drinks in hand, having regained her composure somewhat.

"Where's Boomer?"

"I left him with my parents. I thought it would be best."

"I'm sorry you had to do that. He's a beautiful dog."

"It's okay." It wasn't exactly okay, but he'd table that issue for now. "I almost forgot. I've got something for you." He leapt up, went to his jacket, and pulled a small gift box from his pocket.

As he sat down beside Abbie, she shook her head. "Oh, Jack. You shouldn't have. I know people always say that, but I really mean it."

He grinned. "Don't worry. Just open it. It's something I want you to have."

She lifted the lid of the small square box, then she burst into laughter. "Ear plugs! It's the best gift I've gotten this year. Thank you!"

"I thought it might help you block out the coyotes."

"It will. It's just perfect." She pretended to dab a tear.

Jack said, "I know. Those guys in the holiday diamond commercials don't know what they're doing."

Abbie was suddenly serious. "I wouldn't wear a diamond. It's almost impossible to know whether you're buying a conflict diamond."

Jack frowned in confusion. "You mean like a blood diamond?"

"Yes!"

"Oh, well, I'll keep that in mind." He began to grin slyly.

Abbie looked suddenly shocked or horrified—maybe a little of both. "I didn't mean—"

Jack was now completely amused. "I know that, Abbie. Relax!"

She looked sheepish. "It's Christmas. I don't need to get up on my soapbox today. Sorry."

Jack stopped laughing and looked into her eyes. "Don't be. You're aware of what's going on in the world. You have passionate views. Never apologize for that."

She gazed into his eyes. For a moment, he was lost, but she nodded, grateful for his understanding—at least that was how he read it, because otherwise he might think they'd connected for a fleeting moment. Not that he'd mind that at all. She was pretty and smart, but he'd known plenty of pretty, smart women. Abbie was different. The more time he spent with her, the more he wanted to know her. Or maybe he just wanted her.

She set down her wine glass. "So Jack, what are you passionate about?"

He nearly spat his beer out. Think before you speak. "Well... uh... obviously the environment. I am a forest ranger, after all. And people. When I bring a person who's been injured or lost to safety, it feels good to know I've made a difference in someone's life."

Jack thought he saw envy in Abbie's expression.

"I've never felt that way at work."

"But your work is challenging, and you do a good job."

She exhaled. "I guess I do, but it isn't really what I

was expecting." She leaned closer as if she were sharing a secret. "I don't really like it."

Jack shrugged. "Then change."

Her face lit with amusement. "Oh. Okay!"

He refused to relent. "Life's too short to keep doing something you hate."

"I didn't say I hate it. With any luck, I'll make partner soon."

"And you'll suddenly like the work then?"

"I'll feel better."

"Really? But will you be happy?"

"I'll have achieved a huge goal."

"Objection! Nonresponsive!" He added, "I'm not a lawyer, but I've watched them on TV."

"Okay. Yes, it'll make me happy to have ticked off that box."

"Careful, Abbie. Making partner is part of their trap." He was only half joking.

"Okay. You win. I may reassess after that."

"This isn't about winning arguments. It's about winning life." He could see that he'd touched a raw nerve, so he moved on. "So that covers work. What about family? How's the cruise going?"

Abbie chuckled. "I only know what I see on Facebook. They've posted a couple of selfies. Heartwarming." She looked at him wryly.

"And what did they get you for Christmas?"

A look of panic flashed in her eyes, leaving Jack wondering where he'd gone wrong.

She averted her eyes. "A gift card."

Jack nodded with approval. "You can't go wrong with a gift card."

Abbie wrinkled her forehead since, apparently, they'd managed, but she said, "Yeah, it's usually a pretty safe choice."

The evening barking and howling of coyotes commenced. Abbie said, "Ugh. I was hoping I might get lucky tonight."

Jack lifted an eyebrow.

A shocked Abbie said, "I meant the coyotes! The howling."

With anyone else, Jack might have made a remark about being disappointed, but he felt that he had to be careful with Abbie. So he smiled and said, "It's okay. I knew what you meant."

Abbie stared at the fire, deep in thought. "You shouldn't feel as though you have to babysit me just because I've got an issue with certain animals."

Jack wasn't sure how to respond. He wouldn't have done this for any other renter, and she had to know that. He could keep evading the issue and acting as if he were just the nicest guy in the world. But he wasn't. He was here because he liked being with her. He liked how she felt in his arms, and he wanted her soft lips on his. In fact, there was nothing about Abbie Harper he didn't like or want. And the words just slipped out.

"I like you." Well, that was subtle. "And I don't like the idea of leaving you here to suffer alone."

"Jack—"

"Don't worry, I know you're not looking for... well, a—"

"I like you, too."

A moment of stunned silence followed and was about to grow even more awkward, so Jack said, "Well, okay, but don't ask me to go steady, 'cause I'm not that kind of guy."

Her eyes sparkled. "I won't. Promise."

Their amused looks dissolved to flat-out staring. Were her eyes shining? He effected a practically normal smile. "Good. So we'll just take it easy."

"Sounds good." She gazed into his eyes. Intensely.

Then they lunged for each other. And that was the end of the taking-it-easy phase of their relationship. Coyotes chose this moment to howl their approval, which was not necessarily a shining endorsement of Jack's honorable intentions.

His lips brushed hers as they paused for an oxygen break. "Just for the record, you started it."

"I don't think so." She kissed him before he could argue the point.

The haunting sound of coyote howling started up

again. Jack felt like howling himself. He wanted Abbie as he'd never wanted a woman before. Every touch was electric. And she wanted him. If he'd had any doubts, she'd dispelled them when she climbed on top of him and practically pinned him to the sofa. No complaints there. The third round of coyote howling came with some growling. Abbie scrambled off Jack so fast it took him a moment to refocus.

"I'm sorry. That noise—I can't..." She shook her head as she trembled.

Jack slowly bobbed his head, unsure whether to nod with compassion or shake his head and cry out "No!" in desperate protest. Begging wasn't out of the question. "Okay." Sometimes he told little lies. "That's okay." Despite everything he believed about wildlife conservation, he had a momentary urge to go outside and make a certain species extinct. Instead, he put his arm about her shoulders and comforted her. And when she had calmed down, his mind strayed to practical matters. Coyotes outside were one thing, but he had a dog that liked to spend time inside the house. How was that going to work out? Assuming this did.

JACK WOKE HER. She'd fallen asleep on his shoulder. She brushed her hair from her face and looked up at him. Every time she saw those gentle eyes looking at her, she lost a little more control, and worse, she no longer cared. He was unlike anyone she'd known, which wasn't all that surprising. She'd spent the past several years around lawyers. It wasn't the most diverse sample.

He shifted his position on the sofa. "I've got work tomorrow, so I was thinking tonight I should sleep in a bed." He hastened to add, "In the second bedroom, I mean."

For someone who didn't do casual sex well, Abbie was unexpectedly disappointed. But Jack was different, or at least her feelings for him were. She was crazy about him—or just crazy.

He stood, so she stood, too.

"Good night, Abbie. Merry Christmas." He hugged her, and she wished him the same. And then he was gone.

She went into the bedroom. The bed looked comfortable. There was always a bright side. And her Christmas Day had been nice—more than nice. It had come so close to perfect and yet missed the mark. She had killed a perfectly romantic evening with her irrational fear of dogs and their cousins, the coyotes. Her heart sank. Why couldn't she have a fear that was normal—like a fear of spiders? Who wouldn't understand that? Or a peanut allergy? People managed to work around those. (For starters, peanuts don't bite.) But she was cursed to be a single woman with a fear of man's best friend.

She pulled down the duvet and fluffed up the pillows a little too vigorously as she thought back on the evening. It had all gone south so fast. One minute, they were contenders for the tonsil hockey Stanley Cup, and the next, she was humiliating herself with a near panic attack. She rolled her eyes at herself in disgust. *Yeah, Abbie, guys love that.* She climbed into bed.

*C'mon, put things in perspective. It's not as if it's ruined your life or anything. So it didn't work out. You're from two different worlds. One has hot guys with dogs and the sweet sound of coyotes from the dense, scary woods, and the other has dense, scary lawyers— some of whom also have dogs, but probably only the good-looking ones.*

*Your world sucks, Abbie Harper. And to all a good night.*

## EIGHT

JACK WAS GONE by the time she woke up. No surprise there. He did leave a note. That was nice. Some sort of work crisis had called him away. As excuses go, it wasn't too lame. He'd made a good effort. She respected that.

His early departure left her with a whole morning to drink coffee and eat an apple fritter she'd brought up from the city. She was beginning to enjoy being an inert mass.

As the morning wore on, she found herself looking outside and wanting to get out and about. Being cabin bound gave her too much time to think. She resisted the impulse to pull out her computer and phone and get sucked back into work mode. Instead, she turned on the TV to get caught up on the news. It had been a quiet holiday, crime-wise. Even criminals liked a good meal and some presents. A couple of teens had gone cross-country skiing yesterday afternoon and hadn't returned home all night. That didn't sound good.

A motor outside turned out to be, as she'd hoped, a snowplow. In a few minutes, she would be free. She turned off the TV, got dressed, and tidied up until the driveway was clear.

As she drove into town, her first goal was to get gas. Next she went to the store for provisions (more wine). Her last stop was for groceries. While she waited in line, she overheard the man in front of her talking to the teenage girl ringing him up. They were talking about the lost skiers. The clerk, who looked high school-aged, knew both teens. They hadn't been found yet. Abbie looked at her watch. It was past ten o'clock. They'd been gone a long time.

Then the clerk mentioned Jack. Apparently, the clerk was privy to nearly as much information as the dispatch operator. Everyone came into this store at some point in their day. The man left before Abbie could manage to strike up a conversation. She sucked at initiating conversations with strangers unless she was wearing a suit. It came with the job, but being outgoing was not natural to her. With the customer gone, she turned to the checker with a questioning look. "You mentioned Jack Whelan."

"Yeah, you know Jack? He went out with the team. Fingers crossed they'll be back soon."

"Yes, fingers crossed."

Abbie walked out to the car, stunned by the news. Why hadn't it occurred to her that Jack could be involved? He'd left before she woke up. He must have gotten the call in the night. She looked up the location of the ranger station on her phone and went there to ask about Jack. Inside was a woman, probably in her forties, with long hair twisted tightly in a knot at the nape of her neck. She greeted Abbie. They were in a large room full of desks and cubicles. Men and women in police and ranger uniforms were engaged on the phone, studying maps on the wall and computers, and quietly talking with grim looks on their faces.

"I'm here about Jack Whelan. He's a forest ranger."

"Yes, I know Jack."

"I was wondering how he is."

The ranger squinted. "Are you family?"

Abbie's eyes widened. "Why, has something happened?"

"No. I'm just not at liberty to share information about an ongoing operation."

"But everyone else in town seems to know what's going on." Abbie's stomach started churning. Of course they wouldn't share details with random strangers who wandered into the building. It made sense to her lawyer brain, but her heart wasn't nearly as logical. "I understand. I do. I'm sorry, my name's Abbie Harper." She extended her hand, and they shook. "I'm renting his cabin."

"Oh, Abbie." Her eyes registered some sort of recognition. "I've heard your name mentioned."

Had she? That caught her attention, but she was too concerned about Jack to give it any more thought. "I've gotten to know him a little, so when I heard about all this, I was worried."

The ranger smiled warmly and lowered her voice. "He's okay as far as we know. That's all I can tell you."

Abbie understood but was disappointed.

The ranger walked her to the door. "I'll tell him you were asking about him."

Abbie shook her hand again and thanked her. On her way to the car, she reminded herself he was okay so far.

When she arrived back at the cabin, she checked the TV news and then pulled out her phone, following what news she could find via social media. Most of what she heard were rumors, with occasional quotes overheard on police scanners. She was fixed on it, nevertheless, and sat reading and worrying well into the night.

The coyotes were at it again, so she put in the

earplugs Jack gave her. Jack could be hurt, and no one would tell her. Why would they? She was only a renter who'd known him for three days—just a so, so single woman obsessing over a man she just barely knew. How much could she feel after so little time? She wouldn't answer that, because these were the workings of an unbalanced mind. She fell asleep counting the reasons why she needed to get a grip.

ONE OF TWO skiers had lost her balance on a downhill slope, veered off the trail, and tumbled over a cliff. She landed on a ledge twenty feet down. Her knee and right arm were injured and probably broken, so her ski partner went to get help. By the time he returned with a rescue team, the strong wind had blown the snow into drifts, and darkness had fallen. The last place the skier could identify was the trailhead. With night-vision goggles, they searched an expanding perimeter for an hour before they finally found the injured skier.

Blowing snow stung Jack's face as he rappelled down an icy cliff face to the snowy ledge where the skier had fallen. He rendered first aid and carefully lifted her into the litter they'd lowered down with him. At Jack's signal, the team above began hoisting her up.

As Jack steadied the basket, a strong gust of wind blew it against his head and threw him off balance. He took a step to recover, but the ice broke off beneath him, and he fell off the ledge.

He hung suspended by a rope while his colleagues got the injured skier to safety. Next, they pulled Jack up until he was safely on solid ground. Halfway down the mountain, the helicopter took off to take the injured skier to the hospital.

Jack stood up and dusted the snow from his jacket. As they headed back to their snowmobile at the trail-head, his friend Mason said, "Don't do that again."

"What, get thrown off a ledge? I'll try not to."

"No. Don't make me lift like that. Dude, eat a salad."

Jack smacked Mason's chest with the back of his hand. "It's called muscle."

Mason rolled his eyes, and the two laughed and rode back to the ranger station together. A phone call came in from the hospital. The skier they'd rescued had a broken kneecap, a rib, and an arm, but she was going to recover.

Jack smiled at Mason. "It's a good day in the mountains." As he headed for his desk, one of the rangers approached him. "Jack, you had a visitor earlier."

"Oh?"

"Abbie Harper."

"Abbie?"

"She said she was worried." Jack ignored the twinkle in the ranger's eyes and thanked her. He called the cabin, but there was no answer. Now *he* was concerned. He got permission to leave a half hour early. He couldn't imagine what would worry her so that she'd come looking for him. He tried calling again but no answer. Every crime scene and accident he'd ever encountered started coming to mind.

"C'mon, Abbie. Pick up." He drove as fast as he safely could. Boomer was still at his parents', so he wouldn't need to be walked. The poor dog would miss Jack, but he'd survive.

Jack turned into the driveway, which was plowed, as he'd arranged. A minute later, he was at the door, knocking. No answer. He knocked again and called out her name. Her car was in the driveway, cleared of snow, so she'd made it back home from town. Lights were on, and he heard the TV.

"Abbie!" He looked through a gap in the curtains and saw her slumped over on the sofa. He knocked and called to her again. Then, with cold fingers, he fumbled to enter the key code, then opened the door.

"Abbie!" He rushed to the sofa. He could see she was breathing. He checked her pulse to see if it was normal.

She bolted upright and cried out.

"Abbie, it's me."

She came fully awake and looked at him. "Jack!"

They flew into each other's arms, and Jack held her against him. "What happened? I've been trying to reach you!"

She pulled out the earplugs he'd given her and looked up at him, concerned. "Are you okay?"

He shut his eyes and smiled to himself. "The earplugs."

Her face lit up. "They're fantastic! Between the earplugs and the TV, I barely heard the coyotes! But you! I heard you were involved in the rescue of that poor skier."

"She's going to be fine. Busted knee, a cracked rib, and a broken arm, too. But they'll heal."

"Well, I'm glad, but I was worried about you!"

"Me? I was just doing my job. Nothing to worry about." He shook his head and dismissed the idea.

"What happened here?" She reached up and touched his forehead.

He winced but quickly smirked to disguise it. "Oh, that. I just bumped my head at work."

"Fighting with file cabinets again?"

"Something like that."

Her eyes were so soft, and her lips even softer, he had to focus on what she was saying. "So what happened? The news said she fell off a cliff. She must have been terrified."

"I imagine she was."

"And the rescue! Was it very dangerous?"

"Everyone there was well trained. They just did their jobs."

"Are you sure you weren't in danger?"

"I'm in danger every time I get into a car. But I don't sit around wringing my hands over it."

"Well... no, I guess not."

She still looked troubled, and it secretly pleased him to know that she cared. He said, "It didn't occur to me that you'd be worried."

"Well, maybe I care about you."

He gazed into her eyes. He wanted to tell her it surprised even him how much he cared about her, but he didn't want to scare her away.

The eleven o'clock news came on the TV, and they led with the story of the fallen skier. Abbie turned to watch. It showed rescuers carrying the litter to the rescue helicopter, which then whisked her away to the hospital. Jack was nowhere to be seen since, at the time, he was still being pulled up from the ledge.

"So you really weren't in the middle of it, risking your life?"

He grinned. "Look at me. I'm fine." He stepped closer. "And I'm here." He put his hands on her shoulders. "And I'm glad to see you." She gazed back at him with unguarded eyes. His eyes trailed down to her lips, and he kissed her.

She wasn't flinching or pulling away, so there might be hope for him, after all. He kissed her again, and he held her and stroked her smooth hair. She was so soft and warm, and she fit against him as if she were meant to be there. His heart swelled with a feeling for her that was beginning to have a life of its own. It was taking control of his logic. Stranger still, he was about to let go and allow it.

AFTER WORRYING about Jack for most of the day, Abbie felt so relieved to see him that her good sense went out the window. She forgot to think about what she was risking to let herself fall for a guy she wouldn't see after this week. All she thought of was how good it felt when she was with him. Attraction was not a strong enough word to describe what she felt. Yes, he was insanely attractive—not like the refined sort of men she so often saw in the city, all fastidiously groomed and fitted with suits, with the same haircuts and mani-cured hands. No, Jack was broad shouldered and rugged. His hair always looked a bit tousled, his hands were all rough, and he smelled like, well, Jack. It was her new favorite scent.

Without saying a word, she took his hand and led him into the bedroom. She sat him down at the edge of the bed and bent down to unlace his boots.

With a light chuckle, Jack said, "Careful. Those feet could be a deal breaker."

She laughed as he pulled her up by the elbows. She used the leverage to push him back by the shoulders until he was on his back. She could not kiss him enough, which was good, because he kissed her back, nearly senseless. With one move, he pivoted her to her back and thoroughly kissed her. He turned and got out of his boots faster than she'd thought humanly possible, and he climbed back into bed, where he lay on his side, resting his head on his hand. "Abbie Harper." He gazed at her.

She was in trouble. And all she could think after that was that she didn't care. He leaned over and pressed his lips to hers. And that was the last time she bothered with thinking for the rest of the night.

Until she went to retrieve her emergency condom supply. She was surprised that they hadn't expired. It had been that long since she'd dusted off her vagina and taken it out for a spin. But they were good. It was all systems go until she returned to find him asleep. She nudged his shoulder. Nothing. She took a more vigorous tack. He was dead to the world. The poor guy was out cold.

On the plus side, the coyotes seemed to have moved on to some other locale. So she was finally going to have that nice, quiet night's sleep she'd been longing to have.

Great.

## NINE

MORNING SUN SHONE through the white linen curtains across the room. Jack rolled over and stretched out his arm, which landed on Abbie's smooth skin. He opened his eyes. As his head cleared, he thought back on everything that had happened—everything until he had gone to bed.

Abbie opened her eyes and rolled onto her side, studying him.

Everything ached. He had been out in the snow for several hours, rappelled down a cliffside, been hit in the head by a litter, fallen off a ledge, been pulled up, and tromped back to the snowmobile... yeah, that sounded about how he felt. But after he'd arrived here, his memory was fuzzy. "Abbie, about last night..."

"You fell asleep."

Although he'd had good reason to stay awake, his

weary body had won out. Now he ached all over and his head hurt, but Abbie was lying beside him. He offered a chagrined apology for falling asleep, then he reached out and brushed his fingers over her neck.

He murmured, "I hope you had the good sense to get a rain check before I dozed off."

She took his face in her hands. "Here's my rain check."

She kissed him, then Jack made sure he paid up to her full satisfaction.

SOMETIME LATER, Jack and Abbie lay spent on rumpled bed sheets. His phone alarm went off, and he groaned.

Abbie snuggled closer. "If you kiss me, I'll make you some coffee."

He pressed his mouth to hers while she moved closer until the length of her body touched his. She loved the feel of his skin against hers.

"Abbie, I'll be late if I don't get up now."

She arched an eyebrow.

"And get dressed. We had a deal. A kiss for a coffee. I believe I've delivered my part of the bargain."

"Have you? I don't remember. Remind me."

He kissed her again, a slow, deliberate kiss that

drew a sigh from her. "Remember that while you're making that coffee."

Abbie gave him a slightly tortured smile and got up. Slipping into last night's sweater and jeans, she went to the kitchen.

Five minutes later, Jack emerged fully dressed and in a rush. "I just got a text from work. No time for coffee." He gave her a quick kiss and paused just long enough to look into her eyes and shake his head. "Abbie Harper..."

ABBIE SPENT the next several hours trying to come back to earth. Her head spun when she thought about Jack, which was not a good thing. But since it was how things seemed to be, she simply suspended her good sense and logic for the rest of the week.

She went into town and walked about, did some shopping, took a phone call from a client who, evidently, had even less of a life than she. She returned home in a new state of mind. Even without Jack, being here in the mountains did that for her. It was peaceful and so far removed from her usual life that she felt like a better version of herself.

Her phone rang. That, alone, was amazing. She must have been standing in just the right spot.

"Not even a text? Either something is terribly wrong, or you're happy."

"Choice B. And a merry Christmas to you, too."

Taylor laughed.

"So how was your Christmas?" asked Abbie.

"Oh, you know. The usual. Gifts and relatives swirling about in a vortex of holiday cheer. Oh—and the food! Ugh. We've got some work ahead of us now."

"We? Speak for yourself. I've been pretty good about food up here."

The silence lasted so long that Abbie pulled the phone from her ear to make sure they hadn't been disconnected.

Taylor's voice dropped half an octave as she spoke with her "don't mess with me" voice. "Okay, what's going on?"

Now it was Abbie's turn to be silent.

"No! You did not!"

"Didn't what?" Abbie was truly confused.

"You've met a man!"

Abbie lowered her voice, as if someone might hear her inside the cabin. "How did you know? Can you tell from my voice?"

"No. The food."

Abbie shut her eyes for a moment. "Oh."

Taylor said, "No one is 'good about food' over the holidays unless there's a man."

"Okay. You got me."

"Well?"

Abbie gave her the basic facts—their meeting, his looks, and how she might possibly find him attractive.

Without missing a beat, Taylor said, "You've slept with him, haven't you."

*Busted.* "Uh... I gotta go. I left something on the stove."

"Abbie?"

"Merry Christmas! Talk to you soon!"

"Abb—"

Abbie pressed the red button. She couldn't believe she had done that to Taylor. But she had guessed her way far beyond anything Abbie was ready to divulge to the world. Not that Taylor would utter a word to a soul. But she'd know, and then she would want to know more. She would want to discuss it, and Abbie wasn't ready to talk about it yet, mainly because she didn't know what "it" was yet.

Taylor called back once and then left a few texts.

Abbie texted her back. "I'm fine. It's just too soon to talk."

"At least give me a name."

"Bob."

"Yeah, right."

"Oh, you meant HIS name???"

"Okay, I give up. Talk to you soon."

Abbie smiled. As if she'd give Taylor his name. That woman could research her way through the most Byzantine web of corporate intrigue and deceit so fast, she could make a CEO's head spin. Give her a name? Sorry, no.

ABBIE WENT to the fridge and stared at its contents. She'd thought maybe Jack would call during the day, but he hadn't. She looked at her watch—after seven. Okay. If he'd wanted to take her to dinner, he would have called her by now. Had she been out of practice so long that her expectations were way out of line? Apparently so. Still, she wasn't desperately hungry quite yet. So she poured a glass of wine and grabbed a couple of crackers.

Which she promptly set down. *Who're you kidding?* She pulled out the leftovers. Mashed potatoes, turkey, dressing... she was on her third shoveled spoonful when a knock sounded at the door. Her eyes opened wider than she'd ever imagined they could. She made an effort to close her mouth. Unsuccessful. What happened next wasn't pretty, but—

Another knock sounded.

"Abbie?"

"Wmgh-wmgh!" (*Coming!*)

As she wiped her face and checked her reflection in the microwave door, she made a mental note not to use that dish towel again. Then she went to the door, paused to breathe in and out three times, and then opened the door.

"Jack! Hi!" It was meant to sound casual. Whether it actually did was debatable. But the sight of him dazzled her so much, she didn't even care.

"Hi, Abbie." He stood smiling.

"Hi, Jack." She smiled back.

His smile went crooked. "Mind if I come in?"

"Oh! Sorry! Yes—I mean, no!" She opened the door. *Turns out, love makes you stupid—the definitive answer. Did I say—I mean, think—love? I meant hormones.*

Jack looked endearingly hesitant as she invited him in and led him to the sofa. He sank down with a deep sigh. Abbie brought him a beer. "Enjoy. It's your last."

He made a face of feigned panic.

Abbie shrugged. "It's the last one I've got, anyway."

He held out his hand and gently pulled her to the sofa beside him. "How was your day?"

Abbie began to reply, but he kissed her. Well, okay. She had nothing to add to that.

"You were probably going to ask me how my day was."

Abbie thought she might have if he'd given her half

a chance, but he'd kissed her instead, so she had no complaints. "So how was your day?"

"Ugh, don't ask." The glint in his eyes was more effective than she'd ever let on.

"Rough day pushing that pencil?"

He gave a pained nod. "I had to get up and sharpen it twice."

Abbie's jaw dropped. "Oh, the humanity."

He was surprisingly good at appearing pathetic.

"What can I do to help?"

In an instant, his expression turned mischievous. "Well..."

It took her one second to respond. "Okay." She leaned over to kiss him while he pulled her closer.

A couple of kisses later, he said, "Actually, I was wondering if you'd go out with me this evening."

"On a date?"

"I guess you could call it that." His indifferent attitude dissolved when he searched her eyes.

Abbie thought she might melt. "Yes, I would love to."

His eyes lit with genuine pleasure, which caught her off guard.

All she managed was the same old ridiculous smile she seemed to have had on her face since he'd arrived— or since she'd met him, for that matter. "Wait here. I'll just be an hour."

When his brow creased, she rolled her eyes. "Well, okay—a few minutes."

Abbie had perfected the art of slathering on makeup during her first legal clerkship, when she'd had to start looking like an adult. By the time she emerged from her bedroom in a red cashmere V-neck and a fresh pair of jeans and black boots, she was ready for anything this town had waiting for her.

Jack stood when she came through the door. "You look nice."

"Thank you." It came out sounding perky. She inwardly cringed. Jack, however, seemed oblivious to her failure at achieving perfection. He just slipped his hand in hers and led her outside, where his pickup waited.

As he headed down the drive toward the road, he said, "I thought I'd show you my town."

"I'd like that. I've only seen it in daylight. Besides, I'd like to see what it's like from your perspective."

"It's simple. Not at all like what you're used to."

"Which is why I came up here in the first place."

He smiled that same smile—just a little bit crooked —that she didn't think she could ever grow tired of.

What followed was a dinner in the restaurant of a nearby ski resort, where they sat by a roaring fireplace and basked in the warm candlelight glow. Conversation was easy, whether they were laughing or talking about something somber. Their talk flowed from topic to topic in such seamless fashion, she began to wish he'd do something just a little bit wrong so she wouldn't lose herself in her own massive wave of emotion.

After dinner, they went to a bar he sometimes went to after work. When they walked in, he was greeted by a couple of guys at the bar. Jack introduced her, then they went to a dim booth in the back. A half hour later, Mason walked in, followed by a few of their friends. Jack had to have known he might see them there, but he'd brought her here anyway. So he wasn't ashamed to be seen with her in public. Add another point to the plus side. But meeting his friends added pressure to gain their approval.

Someone—not Abbie—suggested they play pool. Jack started to give her a quick lesson on how to play, but she held up her hand. "That's okay. I'll manage."

Jack leaned closer. "It'll give me a chance to wrap my arms around you."

With a glint in her eye, Abbie chalked the cue and said, "Don't tempt me, Jack. You'll throw off my concentration."

Intrigued, Jack lifted his palms in surrender and stepped aside.

By the end of the round, they all knew why she'd declined Jack's instruction. She'd beaten them all.

Jack looked a bit stunned, but no one could tease him, since they'd all lost to her, too.

Abbie put her cue on the rack and then turned to Jack. "I used to play in college to relieve study stress."

Jack's eyes narrowed. "Had a lot of study stress, did you?"

She said modestly, "I played a lot."

Jack went to buy another round. On the way, his boot heel landed on some spilled beer. He slipped but caught himself and regained his balance. His friends cheered his artful recovery. Mason called out, "One fall's enough for this week."

While Jack continued to the bar, Abbie looked at Mason. "One fall? What do you mean?"

"Off the cliff. Didn't he tell you?"

"Uh, no! He fell off a cliff?"

"When he rescued that skier. Jack rappelled down to the ledge..."

Abbie put down her drink. "He rappelled off a cliff?"

Mason frowned with confusion. "Well, yeah. And while we were hoisting her up, the litter hit him in the head and he slipped on the ice and fell off the ledge." He said it with the same urgency one might use to describe taking out the weekly trash.

"He fell off a ledge?"

"Well, yeah, but he had a harness and rope."

Jack returned with a pitcher of beer and sat down while Abbie stared at Mason, slack-jawed.

Mason slapped Jack on the shoulder. "See? He's fine now."

Abbie turned to Jack. "You didn't tell me you fell off a cliff!"

He fixed his eyes on hers with a neutral expression. "Yeah. Well, you seemed kind of worried. Besides, you've told me even less about what you do at work."

"Well, I don't fall off cliffs."

"I was wearing a harness and rope, and the guys pulled me up." He gave his head a slight shake as if it were no big deal.

Mason broke through the tension. "So, Abbie, what's your typical day like?"

Abbie looked at him blankly. "I sit at a computer, print out some papers, make and answer some phone calls, carry some papers around the office, and... I guess that's about it. Oh, and attend meetings, business lunches... dinner at my desk while I work into the evening. Yeah..."

When the silence grew into a large vacuum that threatened to suck any hope of further conversation into it, Abbie said, "It's okay to yawn. I get that a lot."

Jack pulled her to his side. "I imagine you're brilliant and fierce." He kissed her on the forehead.

The talk turned to more entertaining matters, like

New Year's Eve plans. When it came around to Jack's turn to share, he said, "I haven't made any yet, but I was hoping to ring in the new year with my favorite lawyer."

Abbie smiled. "I'd love to. It would be a nice way to spend my last evening here."

Jack said nothing but looked deep in thought. He'd known when she was leaving since he'd rented the cabin to her. Her stay would be up to New Year's Day.

Soon the other three started to say their good-byes for the evening. They all had to work tomorrow, as did Jack. When the last person had gone, Abbie stared at her drink and said slowly, "Hanging... from a rope... off the edge of a cliff."

When Jack remained silent, she lifted her eyes to meet his.

"It's what I do, Abbie."

"Okay."

Abbie finished her drink and then stood and shrugged on her jacket. To his credit, he didn't try to explain or make excuses. It was what it was. She got that. What she didn't get was why she felt tears in her eyes—not enough to pool and fall down her face, but enough to make her eyes blur.

When she finally looked up to see what he was doing during that long, silent gap in the conversation, she found him staring at her. It was a good stare, the appreciative sort that she hadn't received in a long while.

"You're upset."

"You could have died, and I—"

He had an unyielding gaze that unsettled her. "And you—what?"

She was afraid to look into his eyes. "Well... You're a fairly nice person. I guess I might have missed you."

He leaned back and shook his head, smiling.

She took exception to his cavalier manner. "Oh, so you think it's funny that I—?" She stopped herself before she revealed any more. Now frustrated, she said, "Fine. Go ahead and fall off every cliff in the Adirondacks. After that, feel free to work your way down the Appalachian Trail." By now, she was sure he was laughing at her.

But he wasn't. He said, "I'm glad that you care."

She wanted so much to deny it was true. But it was, and she could see that he knew it. She looked into his eyes, and she thought she saw something she felt mirrored there, but neither could voice it—not yet. Jack was different, and that was as much as she dared to admit at the moment.

His eyes crinkled as he smiled. It was more to himself than to her. But Abbie got the distinct feeling he understood what she was thinking.

He reached out and hooked his arm about her

shoulders and pulled her into a hug. "Abbie Harper, you're different."

And now she was sure he could somehow intuit her thoughts, and worse yet, her feelings. But if that was the case, then he knew it would end with the new year.

# TEN

JACK HAD DOUBTS. He stood in the crisp evening air at the front door to his cabin, his hand poised to knock. Then he lowered his hand. Only last night he'd stood here, been given a kiss, and then sent on his way. He couldn't blame her, really. As much as he wanted to be with her, it had gone far beyond having a good time together. With emotions involved, it would never go smoothly again. He'd been through it before, only this time she was the one who'd put on the brakes. That was a first.

So why was he here? He glanced back at his truck and considered whether he should try to sneak away undetected.

The door opened. "Jack? I thought I heard something out here."

"Yeah. I was about to knock."

"Well, come in." She stepped aside, looking all poised and proper.

That made one of them. He stood at the door feeling awkward.

Abbie smiled. "Sit down. Can I get you a beer?"

That caught his attention. She didn't drink beer.

"I bought it for you." Her mouth quirked up at the corner.

"No, thanks. I don't know why I'm here, really. But it's a clear night, and I thought it might be nice to go skating. But now that I'm here—" He looked into her eyes. "Bad idea."

"I haven't been skating since I was a girl."

Jack's eyes brightened. "It's like riding a bike, except you fall more."

Abbie smiled but shook her head. "I don't have any skates."

"We can rent some."

"I don't know, Jack."

He gave her a straightforward look. "I didn't really come here to go skating. I shouldn't have come here at all." Jack combed his fingers through his hair.

Abbie's brow furrowed. He could almost hear her thinking. She said, "When I told you I needed to slow down, it wasn't that I didn't want to be with you." She hesitated. "I'm not good at this."

"At what?"

"It's not you."

"Oh, please don't. Not that." Jack couldn't help but grimace. He knew that speech. God knew he'd given it enough times himself.

Abbie's eyes narrowed. "What? No! That's not it at all!"

He thought he heard a soft groan. "I should go."

She was silent.

"Yeah, I'm gonna go." He turned, combed his fingers uneasily through his hair yet again, and turned back to her. No, there was nothing to say. He just needed to leave.

"Jack, I'm crazy about you. Too crazy. It's that, and what you do—hanging from cliffs. You must carry a gun for a reason, and that scares me. There, I said it."

"To be fair, I don't hang from cliffs every day."

"And I'm going home in a few days. I just don't..." *Want my heart broken.* "Look, I should let you go. Please—before this gets awkward."

Jack burst out laughing. "Before?"

Poor Abbie looked a little unhinged by her own confession. But she had the sort of lost look in her eyes that made men want to write poems. For her sake, and because he felt the same way, he strode to her and planted a kiss on her lips—a kiss she returned with considerable fervor. When he pulled away, mainly for air, she breathed in and sounded as though she might speak, so he kissed her again.

"Jack, I—"

"Don't say it."

"But you—"

He took her face in his hands. "I love hearing you talk. Everything you say interests me. Except this. We do better when we don't talk about us."

"Point taken."

He kissed her again.

An hour later, surrounded by mountains, Jack leaned down and helped Abbie up from the ice. "So, I'm guessing you didn't take study breaks on the rink while you were in law school."

Abbie was already a few yards ahead of him when she called out, "Sorry, Jack. There's no park or reverse —only drive." Jack caught up and kept pace beside her. When she started to waver, he slipped his arm about her waist and steadied her.

"Thank you. But don't expect me to look. If I turn toward you, I'll fall again."

"That's okay. There's nothing to look at here."

"I beg to differ." She started to smile but lost focus —and balance.

Jack spun her into his arms and barely managed to avoid another fall. They stood facing each other in the middle of the ice.

"You were saying?" His eyes shone with amusement. "Something about the view?"

"Begging doesn't suit you," she cautioned, suppressing a smile.

His gaze fixed on hers. "You suit me."

"Good save!" As she said it, her smile faded.

Jack's did, too. "You suit me, Abbie Harper." Their eyes locked, and their lips nearly touched.

A child's voice drew closer. "Daddy, that's Ranger Jack. He came to our school."

Jack turned and said hello to a girl who looked about seven years old. He shook hands with the father, who glanced at Abbie and then back to Jack. After a brief chat, the father said, "Ranger Jack looks busy rescuing skaters. We'd better let him get on with his work." The dad gave Jack a sly grin and whisked his daughter away.

Abbie watched, shaking her head. "That little girl could skate rings around me."

Jack nodded, agreeing. "But if you didn't need my help, I wouldn't be able to hold you like this." He took hold of her waist, gave her a nudge, and off they went.

JACK PULLED the truck into the driveway, where they found an unfamiliar car parked with the engine running.

Without taking his eyes from the car, Jack said, "Do you know who that is?"

"No. I was going to ask you the same."

"Wait here." He started to open the door but turned back and said sternly, "Stay in the truck."

She whispered, "What are you doing? We don't know who that is!"

"That's what I'm going to find out."

She grabbed his arm. "What if they're armed?"

"So am I."

"What?" She backed away from him. "All evening, while we were skating together, you had a gun?"

He nodded, still keeping an eye on the parked car ahead.

"Jack, I think you should know I'm a staunch believer in gun control."

"Well, Abbie, I think you should know that I'm not."

"You can't just walk around with a concealed weapon!"

"Yes, I can, and I do."

She stared at him in horror.

"Abbie, I'm a forest ranger—a police officer of New York State."

She shook her head in disbelief.

"I'm one of the good guys!"

"One of the good guys WITH A GUN!"

"Look, we can debate gun control later. Just wait here, okay?"

She nodded, but she didn't look very happy about it.

He approached the car with care, weapon holstered but ready. He stopped a safe distance away —enough to allow him to aim and fire, if needed. He'd left his headlights on, but night shadows distorted his view. He tapped on the window. "Can I help you?"

A woman woke up and nearly jumped out of the seat.

"Ma'am, would you step out of the vehicle, please?"

She opened the window a crack. "No, thank you."

Both hands clutched the steering wheel, so there was no imminent threat that he could see. "Why are you here?"

"I'm a friend of Abbie's. She's renting this cabin."

Jack called out to Abbie, who opened the window.

"Tell her it's Taylor."

He called out to Abbie, "Do you know a Taylor?"

"Taylor?" Abbie hopped out of the truck and ran to the car. Seeing Abbie, Taylor got out and they hugged.

Taylor cast a furtive glance at Jack and cautiously whispered, "Abbie?"

"Sorry. This is Jack. He's a forest ranger."

Jack reached out his hand. "Nice to meet you."

Taylor gave him a smile and handshake, but her eyes narrowed perceptibly.

Abbie smiled. "We've been skating."

"Of course you have." Taylor's face wrinkled as she scrutinized the couple. "I tried to call, but my phone went dead—like it always does when I forget to charge it."

Abbie laughed. "As if you'd get a signal here. You're so funny. Sorry if we scared you. We didn't recognize the car, so we thought you might be an intruder."

"Oh, this? It's a rental."

Abbie looked from one to the other. "Let's all go inside. Taylor, you look like you could use a drink. I know I could."

Five minutes later, Taylor and Abbie had glasses of wine in their hands while Jack built a fire, with a beer at the ready.

Taylor took a sip of wine. "I was worried about you. You didn't answer my texts."

"Oh, yeah, well, I only get service when I'm standing in the corner of the kitchen just outside of the second bedroom on alternate Tuesdays."

"So... I guess you must be enjoying all this time *alone*... peace and quiet... away from it all." She lifted an eyebrow.

"I am," she said, sounding strained.

Judging by the silences that seemed to crop up unnaturally, Jack wasn't sure if he was better or worse off for having his back to them, stoking the fire.

Abbie said, "Funny story. On my first day here, the furnace broke, and Jack came to fix it. Turns out he's the owner. Well, we got to talking and... here we are."

Jack turned around to catch Taylor giving Abbie a look. If she wore glasses, she'd have looked over them.

"Skating buddies." Taylor smiled with a sparkle in her eye.

"Yeah, something like that." Abbie almost seemed not to notice.

Jack sat down beside Abbie.

Taylor eyed them both and spoke in a light, almost too pleasant tone. "So... what do you do here in the mountains—I mean, when you're not skating and skiing and doing all of that wintery, outdoorsy mountain stuff that I know you love so?" The last part was clearly directed at Abbie, who smirked.

Ignoring her, Taylor turned to Jack and said, "That's all she talks about—winter sports, curling, ridin' that luge... yeah... one day she forgot and wore her snow shoes to work."

Abbie folded her arms and narrowed her eyes.

Jack smiled. "Abbie plays a mean game of pool."

Taylor lifted her eyebrows. "Does she?"

Abbie smiled. "And Jack carries a gun. It's like the wild west up here, with burly men carrying six-shooters."

"It's a Glock 27 Gen4," Jack said with a tolerant smile.

Taylor eagerly asked, "Can I hold your gun?"

Abbie rolled her eyes. "Taylor!"

Jack removed the magazine and racked the slide, ejecting the live round from the chamber.

Her eyes lit up as he handed it to her. "Oh, I like this! Does it come in Barbie pink?"

Jack grinned and shrugged. "I know a guy who could Cerakote it all pink if you wanted one."

"You're kidding! Really? Oh my gosh, I want one!"

Abbie shut her eyes, took a deep breath, and exhaled. Turning to Taylor, she said, "So how was your Christmas?"

## ELEVEN

JACK SAT at the bar in the Moose Antler Tavern with a half-empty beer in his hands. The bar was a thick plank of oak with the bark still on parts of the edge, and what looked like a dozen coats of shellac on the surface. Every vertical surface in the place was paneled with knotty pine boards. Off to the side hung an old pair of crossed skis and a stuffed fish. Above the bar, like some sort of crown molding, was a wall-to-wall row of moose antlers, hence the name of the bar. It was a vegetarian's nightmare that would've horrified genteel city types, but few visitors found their way here. It was a favorite spot of the locals, though, with its chrome-framed chairs with worn vinyl cushions arranged around Formica-topped tables. It had its own version of old-world charm—if that world were lost somewhere slightly past the midcentury.

Mason slid onto a barstool beside Jack. "Got your message. What's up?"

Jack just shook his head. "Her best friend surprised us with a visit."

"Her girlfriend's here?"

Jack nodded at his beer.

"Dude! Step away. That's a force field that'll never come down."

"I know. That's why I left."

Mason studied his friend then leaned back and shook his head. "Oh wow. You're in love."

"I just met her. You can't fall in love in five days."

"Maybe not, but from the looks of you, you're on a downhill run, and there's a tree up ahead with both your initials carved into it." Mason gave Jack a pitying look.

Jack finished his beer and signaled the bartender for another. "I don't fall in love, so let go of that dream."

Mason held up his palms. "Hey, it's not my dream. You're way more fun when you're in between women." He laughed and added, "Not literally. Although I wouldn't mind being in between women right now. Never mind. I'm shutting up."

Jack barely acknowledged Mason's ramblings as the bartender set another beer before him. He took a drink and then gave Mason a sharp look. "It's not love, but... it's... I don't know... different."

"That's how it starts," Mason said glibly.

"Thanks. Remind me of why I called you."

"Because, as friends go, unfortunately, I'm the best you could come up with on such short notice. I know. It's pathetic. But that's just the kind of guy you are."

Jack stared into his beer mug. "Why am I even thinking about this? She's here for the week, and then she's going home. She's got a life in the city. We have nothing in common. That's all she wrote."

Mason grinned and took a drink. "Well, that was easy. Glad I could help." He waited. When Jack failed to respond, he said, "C'mon. Let's forget about this and go play some pool."

"Abbie plays a kickass game of pool."

Mason smirked, grabbed a cocktail napkin, and handed it to Jack. When Jack looked up with a mixture of confusion and annoyance, Mason said, "To dab your tears."

Jack swatted it away, prompting Mason to let out a laugh.

When he calmed down, Mason said, "What doesn't Abbie do well?"

"Skate."

Mason winced. "Oh, that's too bad. For a second there, I thought things might work out for you."

"Yeah. By the way, this isn't helping at all."

Mason leaned on the bar and actually looked

serious for the first time this evening. "What do you want?"

Jack stared straight ahead. "Her."

"Okay. So the next step is to decide how long you want her for. The rest of the week... the rest of your life...? It's something to think about."

Jack heaved a deep sigh. "I don't want to think. Let's just go play some pool." So they got another round of drinks and headed for the pool table. On the way, Jack thought of Abbie. Everywhere he looked, he could see her. But come New Year's Day, she'd be leaving for home, and he'd have to fish or cut bait.

TAYLOR WATCHED the lights from Jack's truck disappear around a bend in the driveway and then turned to Abbie. "So... he's manly!"

Abbie did not hesitate to agree. "Yeah... now that you mention it."

"And he's tall and good-looking."

Abbie furrowed her brow. "Is he?" She managed to keep a straight face for about three seconds before her eyes twinkled and a broad smile followed.

"And he could probably pinch off the heads of half of the firm with the tips of his man paws."

"Good to know." Abbie emptied her glass and held

it out while Taylor refilled it.

Taylor set the bottle down and picked out another chocolate truffle. "Yeah, I'd marry him myself just for that. It would breathe new life into those staid office parties."

Abbie laughed but then stopped abruptly with an alarmed look on her face. "Wait! Who said anything about marriage?"

"I did—joking, and then you did—not joking."

Abbie hastened to defend herself. "Because it's not relevant to this conversation."

A slow smile formed on Taylor's lips. "Touched a raw nerve, did I?"

Abbie's face went through a half dozen emotions on its way from indignant to helpless. "Dammit, Taylor!"

Taylor's eyes softened. "I know. I suck as a friend for not letting you lie to yourself."

"I hadn't even let myself think of a future beyond this week."

Taylor held out the chocolate box to Abbie. "That's the trouble with thoughts—and with feelings, for that matter. Sometimes they just happen without our permission."

Abbie looked downright annoyed. "Well, they can't. He's all wrong for me."

"Are we talking about the same guy?"

"Yes. For starters, he has a dog."

"So that's a point for the pro side."

"Uh, no. That would be a con for me. I'm not exactly a dog person."

Taylor scowled. "Okay, so he's not perfect for you in every single way. Nobody is. That makes him human."

"Human, yes. Right for me? No."

Taylor studied Abbie. "So far, the worst you can come up with is the dog—which, by the way, makes him hot, in my book. Very manly."

"He lives in the forest—and he carries a gun! I don't even want to know what political party he's registered with."

"I could guess," Taylor said, suppressing a grin. "Look, as long as the gun's not in bed—well, hehe, you know what I mean. I mean, it could be a cannon, for all I know." Taylor shrugged.

"Taylor!" Abbie's annoyance gave way to a small snort of laughter.

Taylor leaned closer and lowered her voice. "So, uh... what're we talking here? I mean, does he have to wheel it in like heavy artillery, or is it more of a cute little pocket pistol?"

"Objection!"

"On what grounds?" Taylor demanded.

"On the grounds of shut up!" Abbie hid her smile

as she got up to replenish their wine supply.

When Abbie returned, she handed the bottle to Taylor then sank into her chair with a sigh. "I do like him," she admitted.

"News flash!"

"But it's just one of those things. Maybe if he were in the city, something could happen. But he's not, so it can't."

Taylor's eyes saddened. "But you like him."

Abbie shook her head. "There's just too much in the way."

"How much? On a pain scale of one to ten, with one being persistent throbbing—of your heart! ...or any body part, really—and ten being your heart torn asunder, stomped on, and tossed onto the subway tracks, where it's eaten by rats before an oncoming train comes and flattens what's left, where would you rate Jack?"

"I don't know. I lost track of the question." Abbie might have laughed if she hadn't felt so tormented.

"Okay. Let me rephrase. If he lived next door to you in the city—without a dog—would you knock down a wall to get at him?"

"Load-bearing?"

Taylor looked delighted. "Ah, so you'd consider it. So you like-like him, not just as a friend."

Abbie didn't answer at first. "I'm sorry. I just had a

flashback to sixth grade." She paused then reluctantly said, "Yes, I like-like him... a lot... maybe with a capital L."

"Which L? Like L or love L?"

"There was no love in that sentence!"

"How about your heart?" Taylor looked at her knowingly.

Abbie felt suddenly shy, which just wasn't like her. But she had to answer. Taylor was like a dog with a bone. She was not going to let this thing go. "Okay. I like him. A lot. Could be love. It's too early to tell."

Taylor looked away and furrowed her brow, deep in thought. "Abbie Whelan. Abbie Harper-Whelan. With or without a hyphen? Or—"

"Taylor! Would you stop?"

"You're right. Why not just keep your maiden name?"

"No!"

"I hadn't really thought of you as such a traditionalist!"

"I mean, no, stop talking about it."

Taylor had the look she always had when she'd nailed a point in a crucial exchange of opposing views at work. "I'll take you to lunch tomorrow, and then I'll leave for New York."

"But you were going to stay until the day after tomorrow."

Taylor looked Abbie in the eye. "You need some time with this guy."

"Why?"

Taylor just looked at her with her smirk-mouthed stare that said, "*Really?*"

Abbie clung to the last thread of her argument. "I refuse to arrange my life around a man."

Taylor said, "Ordinarily, I'd agree. But girl? If I were you, I would arrange myself around *that* man."

Abbie shook her head, but she'd lost the argument not only with Taylor, but also with her heart, and she couldn't pretend to deny it. Her eyes grew misty. "It's like he's thrown me off balance, and I can't seem to find my way back."

"Back to where? To alone? Maybe it's time to let go and regain your balance with him."

"I'm not ready for that."

"It's okay. You don't have to be. Just be willing to consider the possibility."

THE NEXT MORNING, Taylor sat across the table from Abbie in a charming cafe in the center of town. Taylor glanced toward the door and abruptly got up. "Be right back. Restroom," she added to explain her sudden departure.

"Hi, Abbie." She turned to find Jack arriving beside her table, which explained Taylor's sudden departure. Jack glanced at Taylor's plate.

"She'll be back in a minute. How are you?" *How are you? You know how he is. You just saw him a few hours ago. How much could he have changed while he slept?*

"I'm fine. Look, I know you're busy today, but I was wondering if maybe tomorrow I could take you to dinner?"

Abbie smiled too much, and she felt as though her eyes were as bright as the Christmas tree in the corner. "I'd like that." She proceeded to lose herself in his gaze. Her mind was officially numb. Not a thought in her head except Jack's eyes, the small lines in the corners when he smiled, and his chiseled cheekbones and full lips.

"Good. I'll call you." He touched her shoulder as he walked away—just like *Brief Encounter*. Of course, her encounter with Jack would be even briefer. Why had he done that—to torment her with romance? She had to admit, it was the perfect gesture. Taylor returned just in time, before Rachmaninoff's *Piano Concerto No. 2* took over her brain.

An hour later, with lunch finished, Abbie hugged Taylor good-bye, and they drove off in opposite directions in their rental subcompacts.

## TWELVE

ABBIE WAS NEARLY OUT of town when the phone rang. She pulled over and answered it.

"Abbie? It's Jack."

"Hi." *Well, that was quick.* When he said that he'd call, she'd thought it would be sometime tomorrow.

"I've got to go out on a rescue. I'm not sure how long it'll be."

"Okay. Well, if dinner doesn't work out—"

"No, it's not that. It's—I hate to ask you this. But my family's gone skiing, and everyone else I could ask doesn't seem to be home. You know, the holidays. Anyway..." He hesitated and exhaled. "It's Boomer, my dog. I was on my way home to feed him, and now... well, I was wondering if your friend, Taylor, could feed him. He doesn't need to be walked or anything. He's got a door he can come in and out of."

"Well, sure, I could call her and ask."

"She's not there with you?"

"She just left, but she can't be more than ten minutes away."

"Thanks, Abbie. I would never have asked you, but I thought maybe Taylor wouldn't mind."

"Oh, no, she loves dogs!"

"Great! You don't know how much this means to me."

Abbie took out a pen and paper and jotted down his address and instructions.

When he was finished, he said, "I gotta go. I'll call you when I get back."

"Okay. Bye."

Abbie spent the next hour trying to call Taylor. No luck. Either she had no signal, or her phone had died. Now what? She'd left a message on Taylor's voicemail, but it didn't look like she was going to get it in time. Jack was counting on her. She could not let him down.

Twenty minutes later, she sat in Jack's driveway while she mustered the courage to enter his house. She looked for a neighbor who might help, but the driveways on either side of his house had not been plowed since the storm. Clearly no one was home. So she sat for another ten minutes. "No! I will not be defeated by this." With that, she opened the car door and headed for the front door.

It was a small one-story clapboard house with a tiny square patch of lawn in the front. She found the key in a lock box that hung from a hook on the side of the porch. Inside, it was neat, for the most part, sparsely furnished, with no art on the walls. It had a temporary look to it that formed a contrast to the warmth of the cabin. She listened for signs of a dog but heard nothing. Catching sight of a dog bed, she stopped. Her heart pounded, and adrenaline burned in her chest. This was crazy. What had she been thinking? She'd been thinking of not letting down Jack, that was what.

The house was silent. She took a deep breath. "You can do this." She hadn't been this scared since the bar exam. Okay. She was inside the kitchen. A pile of mail sat on the counter. Beyond it was a pantry, door open. A drawer by the sink was open an inch. That would get on her nerves. As she went over to close it, a movement outside the window caught her eyes. Boomer. Good, he was outside. She sighed, just a little relieved. "Okay, Abbie. Let's get this done quickly." She refilled the water bowl then found the large bin of dog food Jack told her about in the pantry. She'd just filled the bowl and was about to return the scoop to the bin when the clicking of claws sounded behind her. Boomer ran into the kitchen and straight to his dish. Abbie panicked and stepped inside the small walk-in pantry and pulled the door closed. Although the door wasn't locked, she was trapped just the same.

Her heart hammered against her chest as she gasped for air. Something struck her in the face, and she let out a halfhearted cry. Realizing it was only a string to the ceiling light, she pulled it and switched on the light. "I'm... hyper... ventilating." She looked about for a paper bag but found none, so she focused on relaxing and controlling her breathing.

Boomer whimpered and pawed at the pantry door. That wasn't helping to relax her.

Two hours later, she sat on an overturned bucket with her face in her hands. She had cried. She had tried to call Jack but got voicemail. She sat still and listened to Boomer pace the kitchen floor. At some point along the way, she realized that her heart was not pounding. She'd grown just a tiny bit used to his sounds on the other side of the door. He wasn't barking at her. In fact, he hadn't really barked much at all. At the moment, he sounded as though he might be sleeping. Did dogs snore? Between the two of them, she was clearly the one more alarmed by the other one's presence.

Part of her wanted to open the door and attempt to sneak past him, but she still had this deep-seated fear that the dog would wake up and chase her. Thinking her an intruder, he might even bite her. On the other hand, the longer she stayed here, the more foolish she'd look when Jack did return home. So she went to the door and opened it a crack. Boomer was asleep about four feet away. She opened it further. It squeaked. Boomer woke up and lifted his head. She reached out and tried to say his name, but no sound would come out. Boomer got up and looked at her. Abbie shut the door and took up her post at the opposite side of the pantry.

She thought about trying Taylor again, but by now she'd be halfway home. So she sat on her bucket and pulled out her phone to kill time. Just when she was critically close to winning solitaire, the front door opened.

"Abbie?" The footsteps came closer. "Hey, Boomer! Where's Abbie?"

Abbie stood up and tried to sound casual as she spoke from inside the pantry. "Hi, Jack."

After a moment of silence, during which she imagined a number of possible reactions—none of them good—a door off the kitchen opened and closed, and the pantry door opened.

He looked at her with an expression Abbie couldn't read. "Boomer's in the other room." Then he held out his hand, and she took it.

With forced cheer, as though she weren't stepping out of a pantry she'd spent the last two hours in, she said, "So I couldn't reach Taylor, but Boomer's been fed and watered. So I'm off." But when she took a step toward the door, he held on and pulled her into his arms. "You did this for me?"

"Don't be silly. I did it for Boomer."

"Thank you." He whispered it into her neck, and she melted. "Let's go get a pizza and take it to your place."

And then something about the way he accepted how crazy she was, as if it were perfectly fine, made her want to just stay in his arms. She nodded, her face still buried in his chest. "I'd like that."

A PIZZA BOX sat undisturbed on a living room table, while Jack collapsed on his back in the bed beside Abbie. After they'd both caught their breath, he reached over and took hold of her hand. "Can't you take a few more vacation days?"

She squeezed his hand but said nothing.

"Yeah, what was I thinking? So... New Year's Day... three nights, counting tonight, and... two full days."

She rolled onto her side and leaned her head on her palm while she studied the planes of his face.

"So, Abbie..." He turned to face her, playing with unruly wisps of hair about her forehead. "If you haven't got plans..." His gaze trailed down to her eyes. "You haven't, have you? Because, well, I have to work tomorrow, but then I'm off until New Year's Day. I was hoping you'd pencil me in for... however many hours there are left until you drive away."

At first, she said nothing, and he got a sick feeling that he'd misread the whole situation. But then she nodded. He thought he might have seen her eyes moisten, but she buried her face in his chest before he could be sure. He took that as a good sign.

THE NEXT MORNING, Jack sat at his desk at work, catching up with some paperwork. He wasn't a monk. He'd known a few women. But he'd never felt like this about any of them. He'd always imagined that love would come, quiet and sure, over the course of a long relationship—or perhaps out of friendship. And then he met Abbie and felt as if an Acme cartoon anvil had fallen on him. He hadn't seen it coming, and after it did, it was like nothing he'd ever imagined. In other words, he'd lost his mind.

A wad of paper struck him on the side of his head. He turned to find his friend Mason laughing—but not *with* him.

"What?" Jack asked, annoyed.

"Oh, nothing. It's just that you've been writing 'Mr. Abbie Harper' on your legal pad for the past twenty minutes."

Jack looked down. The pad had a few random scribbles on it but was otherwise blank.

"Ha! Made you look!" Mason laughed.

Jack tore the page from his pad and hurled it at Mason. "Don't you have work to do?" He turned back to his computer with renewed concentration.

Mason was right. He'd spent more time thinking about Abbie than work, which was foolish. In a couple of days, she'd be leaving. Then it would be over. His life would be simple again. So why did that trouble him? What he had was an infatuation. That was it. Evidently, he was emotionally arrested at the age of twelve. On New Year's Day, she would drive away. He'd miss her. Then a few days would pass. And then it would be business as usual. What a relief!

AFTER JACK LEFT FOR WORK, Abbie checked for messages, answered a couple of emails that couldn't wait, and then sat in a chair by the window and looked out at the snow-covered landscape. Everything was too perfect—Jack, for one, made her heart pound, her cheeks flush, and her brain stop functioning—all the earmarks of a full-out Abbie-style crush.

But then, when she was alone and able to think again, too many issues stood out—insurmountable issues. The man carried a gun. It was part of his job. She got that. But he carried it off duty, too. People shouldn't have to carry guns to feel safe. Although she had to admit—to herself, never to him—that she had felt safer when they thought there might be an intruder in their driveway. But what if he'd shot Taylor before finding out she was a friend? But he hadn't because he was a trained professional. Managing such situations was part of his job, and the fact that it was, in truth, made her feel safer. So maybe it wasn't such an insurmountable issue, after all.

But the dog was. Their ability to assiduously avoid any mention of it proved what a big issue it was. There was no question that Boomer was a beautiful dog. She even liked him—from afar. On a leash. Tightly held. Which made her feel like a terrible person. Even worse, it made it painfully certain how wrong she was for Jack. When it came down to it, one of them would have to go, and that dog wasn't leaving. Until now, there had been a tacit agreement that they would not discuss the elephant—or in this case the dog—in the room. To do so would be to admit that they hoped for a future, and this was a roadblock that stood in their way.

Despite that, when they were together, nothing else seemed to matter except how it felt to be with him. And what was the harm in that, really? What she had with Jack was a holiday fling. So why not relax and enjoy a few days with a guy who was handsome, romantic, and fun to be with?

Because what she felt was so far from a light, mindless fling. It was heavy and mindful and full of emotions she dared not identify, because you weren't supposed to feel this way after less than a week.

# THIRTEEN

Abbie sat by the fire, reading a book to escape her own self-induced torture-by-logic. She had thought through this thing with Jack from every angle, three times over. It all came down to one thing: she had let herself feel too much and too deeply. On New Year's Day, she would face the consequences. Still, it was too late to undo what had happened. And maybe she didn't want that at all, for she honestly couldn't regret knowing Jack—not yet, anyway.

For now, she was doing what she had dreamed of when she'd first planned her mountain retreat. All thoughts of Jack aside, she loved this cabin. Her favorite spot was here beside the fieldstone fireplace in a big, overstuffed leather chair and ottoman. On each wall perpendicular to the fireplace, large windows gave the illusion of open space. Firelight cast a warm, flickering glow in the room that seemed to wrap her in its warmth and peace. She had even grown used to the coyotes outside, so long as their howls remained distant.

Her mind wandered to a day in the future when she might be able to buy a small place in the mountains for weekend retreats. And then she remembered she seldom had weekends that didn't include work. Still, she could bring work up here—that was, somewhere like this. Although... maybe Jack would consider renting it to her on a regular basis. No, that was a bad idea. She would just wind up falling in love with him. There, she'd said it—well, thought it.

And that was when Abbie decided that she could never come back. She would simply be setting herself up for disappointment. She had too much else going on in her life, like... well... there was work. So maybe the list wasn't long, but her job easily filled up her life. At least it filled up her time, and wasn't that almost the same?

She had to admit that this week had felt good with no work to consume her. She had made the adjustment with astonishing ease, to the point where she wondered why she worked as hard as she did. She didn't like the work, really. What she liked was a challenge and the satisfaction she got from achieving a goal. She had grown used to the tasks that were required of her, and she did them reliably well, but she saw in her colleagues a spark of enjoyment that she just didn't feel. Even Taylor seemed to enjoy what she did on a level that Abbie couldn't match. Maybe it was time to consider other areas of law for which she'd be better suited. Or maybe she just had too much time to think up here.

A knock sounded. For the first time, she noticed that it had grown dark outside. She got up and went to the door.

Before her hand reached the knob, he said from outside, "It's Jack."

Abbie opened the door and gasped. There he stood with two glasses of Champagne. In the driveway, a small sleigh was hitched to a horse. At the front of the sleigh on each side were two lanterns.

He grinned.

"Jack!" She didn't know what to say.

Stepping inside, he pushed the door closed with his boot and then handed a glass to her and offered a toast. "Here's to one-horse open sleighs."

Abbie took a sip of Champagne, and then Jack took her glass. "Go get dressed for an evening out—as in outside."

Abbie stared, once more unable to voice her astonishment.

Five minutes later, she was in the sleigh beside

Jack, who was tucking a fleece blanket around her legs. He poured something from a thermos into a travel mug with a lid and then handed it to her. "Try this."

Abbie took a sip. "Hot chocolate and... Irish cream liqueur?"

Jack's eyes lit up. "For warmth."

And then they were off. Jack drove while Abbie sipped the hot chocolate. The sky was clear, and a full moon cast an otherworldly glow all about. It was so still that the only sounds they could hear were the horse's hooves on the snowy driveway. Jack took a back road that saw little traffic. It was as though they'd stepped back in time to a world that was simple and good, made of soft shadows and moonlight. How must it have felt to live back then? In her world, she rushed to work and to home and ran errands—all through a constant cacophony. She was part of it. By the end of a day, she felt as though she'd left pieces of herself here and there, which she then had to gather before she could begin a new day.

But up here, she felt settled. Maybe that was how it was not so long ago, really. Jack's grandparents might have known such a life. Even now, all the people she met as she wandered about in the town looked content with their lives and aware of the beauty around them. They weren't staring ahead, minds intent upon their frenzied days and lives. And it struck her that she'd felt more like herself during this one week than she could remember having felt since finishing law school—perhaps even before. She had the overwhelming sense that she'd been lost and had finally found her way back to where she belonged.

Jack put his hand on her knee. "You're awfully quiet."

"It's a good kind of quiet." She looked into his eyes.

"For a city girl, you've taken pretty well to life up here."

She noticed he'd left out any mention of coyotes, for which she was thankful. "It's been a wonderful week."

He pulled over to the side of the road and turned to her. "I agree." And he kissed her. It was gentle and perfect. It made her heart ache.

"Let's go home."

If he hadn't turned and lifted the reins, Abbie was sure she'd have lost it. The way he'd said home sounded right, and also impossible. They were like children playing house for a week, but her feelings were growing more real by the minute. She slipped her gloved hand about the crook of his arm and leaned her head on his shoulder as if clinging to him would steady her heart, which was reeling out of control.

They rode through a patch of mist, then it cleared and the moonlight shone softly upon them. "Abbie."

He said it softly, as though he might say more, but instead, he just rode on.

They pulled up to a house with a barn in the back. Jack's pickup was parked outside. Abbie waited in the idling truck, staying warm, while Jack went to the house and knocked. Out came a man Abbie didn't recognize. Jack shook his hand, and the man unhitched the horse while Jack and Abbie drove out of the driveway.

Once home, Jack put the truck in park and turned to her, searching her eyes. Then he pulled her against him and kissed her. Throughout the sleigh ride, she had felt it, but with this kiss, Abbie knew that somehow things were different between them. They had stepped over a line. How could one kiss convey something like that? But his lips were gentle, and his touch was sure. The tentative newness was gone, now replaced by unafraid yearning to know and grow close at all costs. She couldn't help herself now. Without a word, they went inside the cabin and straight to the bedroom, where, under layers of thick down duvets, they made love. It was a slow and exquisite drowning she would never regret.

## FOURTEEN

JACK SURE as hell wasn't ready to say what he felt, but he knew what it was. Everyone had always told him you just knew, but he'd never "just known" anything—until now. He looked over at Abbie, still asleep, with wild strands of brown hair spread over creamy shoulders. Here was a woman he could wake up with tomorrow and all the tomorrows after that.

Abbie opened her eyes and murmured, "What?"

Jack smiled. "I didn't say anything."

"I could hear you thinking. You woke me up." She looked at him with eyes still full of dreams and then closed her eyes. She may have wanted to drift back to sleep, but he couldn't help touching her lips with his thumb, then he brushed his lips against hers.

Jack whispered, "Twenty-four hours. For this day, there's nothing but us."

The drowsy lovemaking that followed grew fervent as they clung to each touch and each moment as if they could keep time at bay.

*Twenty-four hours,* Abbie reminded herself while she made coffee and Jack scrambled eggs. Why think of tomorrow when today was so perfect?

Jack got a fire going in the fireplace while Abbie set the table. She felt at home in her hoodie and sweats as she glanced at him wearing yesterday's clothes, with his shirt unbuttoned and hair going in all directions. There was no way this guy ever didn't look hot. The feel of his skin against hers flashed through her mind as she stared at this man who made her soul sing. He turned and looked into her eyes as though he'd heard her thoughts. Abbie smiled and looked away to finish setting the table.

They spent the morning sipping coffee and lazily sharing snippets of their lives—childhood scars, school memories, family members, and dreams for the future. At times, aching sadness crept in as she thought of returning to her routine. That life seemed so far away and so empty. She chased the thought away and listened to Jack tell her about boyhood escapades with his friends.

"Speaking of which, I've got a pond hockey game in an hour." Jack got up abruptly.

"Pond hockey?"

He grinned. "Oh, yeah. It's an annual event. You're welcome to play. We did away with the 'no girls allowed' rule when we turned ten, not so much because we were enlightened feminists, but because we realized we liked girls—and a few of them played better than we did."

Abbie laughed and stood to face him. "Thanks, but you've seen me skate."

Jack walked around behind her and fitted his body against hers. "We could play in tandem—like sky divers."

Abbie couldn't help but laugh as he took hold of her wrists and pretended to skate and maneuver an imaginary hockey stick. Then he deftly spun her around in his arms and kissed her. "Goal."

One hour later, Abbie sat on a wooden bench at the edge of Miller's Pond, watching Jack take command of the ice. She had known when they'd skated together that he knew what he was doing, but she had no idea how skilled he was—as were his friends.

"They show no mercy." Jack's sister-in-law sat down beside Abbie with a deep sigh. She was pregnant and clearly feeling every bit of eight months. They'd arrived late, so Jack had only briefly introduced Abbie to his brother, Ryan, and Ryan's wife, Kim.

With her eyes on the players, Abbie said, "They certainly play to win."

"They've always been like that," Kim said, shaking her head. Her straight, shiny black hair was cut in a blunt chin-length bob that shimmered with every move of her head.

"How long have you known them?"

"I can't remember not knowing them. We all grew up together."

"All? So you and Ryan were childhood sweethearts?"

Kim grinned. "Not really. It took me a while to catch on to the fact that my best friend was the one. I was the tomboy of the crew. Still am, really. If it weren't for Junior here, I'd be out there playing with them."

"I guess it must be pretty hard to maneuver."

Kim shrugged. "Oh, I can move well enough, but those guys are brutal. And there's always the chance of a fall, so I've hung up my skates for the season. How 'bout you? Do you skate?"

"Once—a few days ago. Jack tried to teach me, but I'm hopeless."

Kim looked at her frankly. "There's no such thing as hopeless. You just need more practice."

Abbie rolled her eyes. "Well, some people need more practice than others."

"True, but if the end result is the same, who cares?" Kim exuded confidence and optimism, two qualities Abbie admired but lacked. The two watched them play for a few more minutes before Kim said, "Pregnancy has made me a wuss. My heated car seat is calling out to me." She glanced back toward the makeshift dirt parking lot, where the cars were pointed toward the pond.

"It was nice talking to you," Abbie said.

Kim smiled. "I'm sure we'll talk again soon."

As much as Abbie liked Kim, she liked being able to watch Jack undistracted. He was a magnificent-looking man: tall and on the muscular side of lean, with broad shoulders and sinewy thighs, no doubt due to all that climbing he apparently did. When he skated, he embodied a combination of fluid motion and power that was, for Abbie, breathtaking. Added to that, his cheeks were flushed and his eyes were bright with the exhilaration of playing outdoors. And... he wasn't a lawyer. Could the man be more perfect?

"You must be Abbie."

Torn from her lustful reverie, Abbie looked up to find an attractive woman of a certain age holding out a cup of hot coffee. "I'm Maureen, Jack's mother."

Abbie took the coffee cup and extended her hand. "Hi. Abbie Harper."

"Yes, I know. Kim pointed you out."

Abbie smiled and nodded. "Please sit down."

Maureen took a sip and looked out at the game. "I'm sorry I'm late. I slept in a little too late and had to wait for something to come out of the oven before I could leave. Everyone always comes over to the house after the game. We'd love for you to join us."

"Thank you. I'm not sure what Jack's plans are, but I'd love to come over."

"It's become a tradition. They all play like they're thirteen and then come over to the house to nurse their aching muscles and joints with food, drink, and laughter."

Abbie chuckled and sipped her coffee. "Oh wow, this is good."

"Jamaican Blue Mountain. It's a little holiday indulgence." She let out a small gasp as one of the players took a spill. "See that one? That's my Johnny, Jack's dad. He thinks he's in his twenties."

"He doesn't look far from it." Abbie wasn't just saying it. Jack's father was fit and held his own quite well against the younger players.

"Maybe not, but he'll feel far from it tonight." Maureen grinned. "We've done this before. I've got the heating pad ready."

Abbie sat with Jack's mother and watched, content in the crisp mountain air. It was quiet except for the scrape of sticks and blades on the ice and the taunts and grunts of the players. Tips of mountains rose up about them, all covered with snow-laden trees. That guy on the ice seemed to like her as much as she liked him. It all felt so right and so good that she wondered why she'd poured so much of herself into building the life that she had in the city.

An hour later, the game ended. Jack and Ryan lost to their father's team. Jack left the ice and sat beside Abbie to take off his skates. "We all usually go to my parents' house afterward. We don't have to. I know it's overwhelming with all the family and friends..."

"I'd love to."

He turned and looked into her eyes, clearly pleased. "Good."

THE LITTLE GATHERING at the house turned out to be quite an affair. The house itself was a grand three-story waterfront home that looked out on the lake. Every room Abbie saw had a heart-stopping view. The great room was a huge open space with vaulted ceilings and a breakfast bar that looked into the kitchen. Everyone had brought food, which seemed to cover every counter and tabletop. Jack set down the case and several bags of chips that Abbie had carried in, then they turned to greet nearby guests. As Jack introduced Abbie, she did her best to remember all of their names.

It wasn't long before Johnny approached them. "Better luck next time, son."

Jack cast a sideways look at Abbie. "I'll never hear the end of this."

Jack's brother, Ryan, appeared with an extra beer, which he handed to Jack. "Not tonight, anyway."

Johnny clapped his hand on Jack's shoulder and laughed.

As large as the home was, the hockey players, their families, and friends managed to fill it with laughter. There was, of course, the obligatory debriefing of the game, complete with any stories the players could muster to rib each other with. Abbie shooed Kim out of the kitchen and helped Maureen clean up and refill serving dishes.

When they were nearly caught up, Jack appeared and took her by the hand. "Mind if I steal her?"

Maureen smiled. "She's all yours."

Jack led her through the door that led to a study. They went to the window and stood hand in hand.

"Your family's so—"

Before she could finish, he swept her into his arms and kissed her. "Abbie..."

Emotion gripped her throat, and her eyes moistened. Before tears could form, she looked away. She didn't know how to express what she felt without sounding sad or needy. She wanted to marvel at how everyone had welcomed her without expectations or judgment. She didn't understand how she could feel at home with them so quickly, as if she belonged. "Your family's been wonderful to me."

"And why wouldn't they be?"

"Because I'm a stranger, because they obviously adore you and, I imagine, feel protective toward you."

His brow creased as he said, "And why would I need protecting from you?"

*Because we're going to break each other's hearts.*

"Hey, you two! What's going on?" Ryan bounded into the room and then acted surprised. "Oh, sorry. Am I interrupting?"

After giving his brother a death glare, Jack said, "You'll have to forgive Ryan, since no one else will. He's still in touch with his inner ten-year-old younger brother."

Just as Ryan was raising an eyebrow and smirking triumphantly at Jack, Kim walked in, gave Abbie an apologetic look, and clasped Ryan's hand. "Come here, babe. I need your help in the kitchen."

As he was leaving, he said, "Why do you need

help? It's not even our kitchen." Kim playfully smacked the side of his head.

Jack shook his head and then turned to Abbie. "I guess we'd better go back before people start talking."

By the time dusk had cast the lake and mountains in a gauzy gray haze, Jack and Abbie were on their way out the door. They'd been asked how they were spending the evening, and each time Jack had answered, "Together." So by the time they pulled onto the road, Abbie wondered herself.

With no warning, Jack said, "Would you like to go out for dinner and dancing?"

Abbie's jaw dropped, then she winced. "At the risk of sounding clichéd, uh... nothing to wear."

"Good, because we're not doing that."

"Okay..."

"The thing is, Abbie, this is a very small town. No matter where we go, we're likely to run into people I know. And as much as I'd like to prove to the world that I can actually get a pretty girl to go out with me, it's our last night together, and I want you all to myself."

"Good. I feel the same way."

Jack raised his eyebrows as though he were surprised or relieved. She wasn't sure which. "All right, then I just have to stop and pick up something."

## FIFTEEN

JACK PULLED into a restaurant Abbie hadn't noticed before. He insisted she wait in the car, which she did but not without mounting curiosity. He came out carrying a very large box that, having no other choice but the bed of the truck, he placed on the floor at her feet. The next stop was his home.

Abbie said, "Oh! I forgot about Boomer!"

"I didn't. He's on a New Year's Eve playdate with Ryan and Kim's dog. I just need a change of clothes. After spending an afternoon with my post-hockey sweat, I didn't think you'd mind if I showered at your place."

In truth, Abbie didn't mind his sweat, either, which was probably a sign that she was now far beyond hope where her feelings for Jack were concerned.

An hour later, they were back at the cabin, having

showered together. Apparently, he'd felt she needed a second shower for the day, and in truth, she hadn't put up much of a fight. They were now by the fireplace, sipping Champagne and dancing to a playlist of Jack's in jeans and sweaters, while the warmth from the fire dried their damp hair. When they were all danced out, Jack left Abbie on the sofa with a throw blanket and instructions to stay out of the kitchen. After some clinking and clanging about, he emerged with lit candles, flatware, and napkins, which he set on the table. These were followed by two thick slices of prime rib, baked potatoes, and asparagus. He put on quiet holiday music, and they quietly ate, content whether conversing or silent. After dinner, they decided to save dessert for later and decamped to the sofa. One movie later, it was closing in on midnight. Jack pulled Abbie off of the sofa. "C'mon, get your boots on. We're going out."

"What? Where?"

"You'll see."

So they went outside and discovered it had snowed lightly. A fresh snow coated the old snow, making everything magical. Once they were in the truck, Jack headed into town.

"I thought you didn't want to go where anyone might see you."

"They won't."

The lakeside was lined with parked cars. Jack pulled into a private drive.

"Who lives here?"

"Some people I know. I rescued their son a couple years ago. Don't worry. I've got their permission. No one's going to come out with a shotgun or anything."

The drive was, in fact, a boat launch, which was plowed down to the dock. They parked there, and a few minutes later, fireworks began.

Abbie sighed. "Oh, Jack!"

Parked as they were in a secluded driveway, it was as if the fireworks were meant just for them.

He smiled at her and slipped his hand into hers. Whether it was the fireworks or Jack, Abbie was thrilled. The fireworks display was stunning and had followed an evening that was intimate and, well, perfect. And now she would simply stop thinking.

BUT MORNING EVENTUALLY CAME. Abbie stood by her car as Jack loaded her bags.

"Will you answer my calls?" Jack gave her that crooked grin that she loved.

"Maybe." She tilted her head and looked up, but her smile quickly faded.

He put his strong arms about her. "If you don't, I'll just have to drive down and see you in person."

A smile bloomed, lighting her eyes. "I wouldn't put it past you, Jack Whelan."

His gaze was intense. She was not prone to swooning, but when he bent down to kiss her, she thought she just might.

"Next weekend in Saratoga Springs."

"I hear it's romantic this time of year."

"It will be next weekend." He kissed her again and leaned on the roof of her car as he closed the door for her.

NEXT WEEKEND DIDN'T COME. Abbie's boss dumped a new project on her desk upon her return to the office, but she'd worked late nights all week to clear her desk enough to take the weekend off. She was all packed and ready to catch a cab to Penn Station, when she got a text from Jack. An elderly woman had wandered off, and he had to go help with the search.

The following weekend, despite her best efforts, she couldn't catch up. She was buried in work, with a layer of pressure above that. She tried to protest, but Bradley dangled the partnership over her head, and she caved and stayed home.

On the third weekend in January, they finally met. Abbie stepped onto the train platform at Saratoga Springs. There he stood, looking so handsome, she just stopped and stared at him. He was real, and his arms felt so good around her. They stared again for a moment before Jack grabbed their bags and they headed for his pickup truck. The hotel was seven minutes away—not that Abbie was counting. Just holding his hand on the way made her heart pound. As soon as the bellhop left the room, they were together, embracing. She breathed in his scent and clung tightly to him. It felt a bit strange to be together again. Since they had met, they'd spent more time apart than together. Jack took things slowly and gently while Abbie rediscovered his face, those amazing lips that she'd daydreamed about when she should have been working, and his body. She reveled in the feel of his skin, his powerful shoulders and long arms and limbs, and the feel of his bare skin against hers as their bodies met and fit together as if they'd always been meant to be one.

Saturday was everything Abbie had longed for, and yet, as the day went on, their conversations grew shorter and farther apart. Being away from their respective homes put their relationship in relief, which would have been perfect if everything else had been in order. For Abbie, it was not. She had had doubts before, but this weekend together had cast a painful clarity on the contrast between how perfect they were together and the impossible obstacles that stood in their way. Still, she fought to hold on, for she knew now that this could be the closest she might ever come to love. Whatever decision she made would bring her to a major turning point in her life, which she'd look back upon and either regret or rejoice over. So she put it off. It was not hard to do. Jack was rugged, good-looking, attentive—everything a woman could want. And she did. She wanted him—physically, emotionally—but then there was logic. All the practical reasons they couldn't be together... well, those could wait until later.

The next afternoon, they would part and go back to their separate lives until the cycle repeated itself. Thoughts of parting hovered about, ever-present but never discussed. After all, what was there to say? So they spent Saturday evening drawing close to fend off the sorrow of parting, which was not nearly as sweet as Shakespeare would have had them believe.

Once again, they stood next to Jack's pickup truck and bade each other good-bye. Abbie slipped her arms about Jack's waist. He was so masculine, she could almost breathe it in as she buried her face in his chest. Then she lifted her eyes to meet his. They kissed and held onto each other as long as they could, then Abbie had to go into the station. At the door, she turned back for one last look at Jack, and then she went inside the train car and back to real life.

DISHES AND GLASSES clinked in one of Abbie and Taylor's regular lunchtime haunts. The two sat across from each other in a booth as a busy waiter set down their plates and was gone just as quickly.

"So how was it? I've been waiting all morning to hear." Taylor dug into her salad while watching Abbie with eyes bright with anticipation.

Abbie smiled faintly. "It was perfect. He was perfect. Agh! If only he didn't make my heart alternate between stopping and pounding whenever I'm with him..."

"Sounds like you need a cardiologist's help more than mine."

Abbie laughed. "I know. It's all body chemistry and hotness, but then—in my sane moments, rare though they may be—I wonder how we could ever make our lives work together."

Taylor nearly dropped her fork. "Whoa, girl! Lives working together sounds like you're talking—you're not... I mean, Abbie... living together? Or the M word!"

"No, we're not talking about it at all. But it's there. Palpable."

Taylor stared for a moment then looked down at the table. "Wow." Then she looked up, puzzled. "I'm usually pretty good at issue spotting, but you've got me here. The man's smokin' hot. He's a nice, decent guy. He saves lives, for God's sake. He's crazy about you. And, best of all, he doesn't wear a damned suit to work —but he'd look hot in one if he did. Yeah, I can see what you mean. A girl would have to be crazy to get mixed up with that!"

Taylor always had a way of forcing her to lighten up, but this time Abbie's laugh came and went quickly. "And... he's a forest ranger. He hates the city. And our law firm doesn't have a branch in the forest."

Taylor chuckled. "Yeah, the only branches there are attached to the trees."

Abbie barely reacted. "He lives in a gorgeous setting, where the towns are all charming, but none of them have work for me."

"Have you talked about it?"

"No! We're not there yet. But we're about a heart-beat away from it. And I think I'm just setting myself up for an ugly heartbreak."

Taylor had the same narrow-eyed look she usually reserved for cases with fact scenarios that just didn't smell right. "Shouldn't you take a breath and maybe wait and see if things can't be worked out down the line? I mean, don't they have park rangers in the city? There must be some sort of work he could do here."

"If he wanted to, but it wouldn't be what he loves doing. He loves his job and all that outdoorsy wilderness stuff. And I—"

Taylor held up her palm. "Hold it right there. If you're about to tell me that you love your job, save it for someone who'll believe it. I know better."

Abbie's brow creased, and she sounded defensive. "I have worked all my life to become a lawyer. When I graduated from high school, I wrote down on a sheet of paper that I was going to go to law school, pass the bar, and become a partner in a New York City law firm. I've got one more step to go to achieve what I've dedicated my life to for years."

Taylor said softly, "I know. I'm simply suggesting that maybe you've mentioned once or twice that you're not really happy."

"Everybody says that."

Taylor smiled, conceding the point. "But you mean it."

Abbie's voice came out a bit harsher than she'd meant it to be. "I'm where I need to be. Jack is where he needs to be. End of story."

Taylor looked worried, as any friend would. Abbie loved her for that, as well as for her current silence.

## SIXTEEN

On their second Friday together in Saratoga Springs, Jack tipped the bellhop then turned to find Abbie sitting on the edge of the bed. When Jack sat down beside her, she stiffened. Something was wrong. He had sensed it the moment they'd met at the station. But when she gently pressed his arm to keep him at bay, his eyes sharpened.

Unable to look into his eyes, Abbie rose and went to the window, where she stared out and spoke without looking at him.

"I can't do this. I didn't want to tell you over the phone."

"Abbie." He wanted to argue or go to her and grasp her shoulders and force her to face him.

"I'm sorry. I know that there's something—we've got something."

He couldn't believe it. It was like an out-of-body experience to hear what came next. She launched into a speech he'd been saying for years, in one version or another. He knew it so well—

Until she said, "If I see you anymore, I'll fall in love with you. And I can't. Because it's not going to work."

He got up and went to her. He couldn't help himself. "Abbie..." Apparently, he was reduced to one-word utterances comprised of her name. Since words escaped him, he held her. She let him, which seemed good at first, until she pulled back enough to look into his eyes, and he saw hers filled with tears.

She said, "Maybe if we lived closer together..."

He looked into her eyes, hoping he might find the Abbie who used to want him. "It's not forever—or at least it doesn't have to be."

She looked back with nothing but doubt, then she went through the list of bad timing, different locations and lifestyles. Then she started on the issues that drove them apart—gun control, for one—and careers. Not to mention the dog!

When she'd gotten it all off her chest, he said, "Abbie, let's think about this."

"What do you think I've been doing?"

"I don't believe that it's not going to work. We haven't given it a chance." He lifted her chin so she had to look into his eyes, and she weakened. Her eyes softened, and it gave him hope. "Abbie, I want it to work. Don't give up."

She shook her head but with less determination. "It's all happened so fast."

He said, "I agree. We need time." She looked away, but he touched her cheek and turned her face toward his, and he kissed her. "Give it a chance."

"Jack, I don't know."

He held the back of her head as she leaned into his embrace. "Just give me one week. Think about us, and how good we are together, and how good we could be. And then next week we can talk."

Despite the hopelessness in her eyes, she said, "Okay."

They clung to each other now, relieved to have postponed their parting. Jack avoided further talk on the subject of them, but he thought about what she'd said. If she knew she was falling in love and believed that they couldn't be together, he supposed it made sense for her to break it off to avoid deeper heartache. Too bad Jack hadn't been quite as cautious. He was already in love.

Abbie got up and packed the next morning after spending a bittersweet night together that both knew could be their last. By morning, they were closer than ever before, and any heartache that followed would be even deeper.

They went out to Jack's pickup and stood, both reluctant to take the next step. There she was, wanting to avoid heartache, and here he was, wanting the same but by opposite means. No matter who got their wish, someone's heart was going to break.

The following Thursday found Abbie at work, her eyes fixed on the computer monitor. She flinched at a knock on her office door.

Taylor held out a business card. "It's for your dog issues."

Abbie halfheartedly thanked her and set the card down on her desk.

Taylor glanced at the card. "She's had a lot of success helping people get over their fear of dogs. Most of her clients have been cured within weeks."

Abbie nodded. "So what's new with you?"

"Oh, not much. Well, except tonight's the night I'm meeting the son of my mother's friend for drinks after work." She made a face that Abbie could not help but laugh at. "So, yeah, another one for the books."

"Sometimes blind dates work out."

"Name one." Taylor folded her arms and leaned back.

"Well, I mean, off the top of my head, I can't name one. But it's got to have happened."

"And people win the lottery. You're right. This could be the one!" She grinned and leaned forward. "So just in case, I wore my lucky red suit."

Abbie nodded, approving. "He hasn't got a chance. So tell me about him."

"Hmm... Let's see. He's got a mother. And a pulse."

"He sounds perfect for you!"

"I know!" They laughed, and then Taylor eyed Abbie. "Are you still on for tomorrow?"

"With Jack? Yeah. For now."

Abbie's cell phone rang. "It's him."

While Abbie answered her phone, Taylor crept out of the office, closing the door gently behind her.

"Hi. I got your message."

"Yeah." Abbie scribbled absently on her legal pad.

"You sound busy."

"Do I?" She knew what he heard wasn't business. It was the strain in her voice. She could hear it herself.

"I can call back."

"No. Jack, I, uh... I called because I can't meet you tomorrow. I'm just buried at work."

He was silent for so long, Abbie thought the call had been dropped. "Jack?"

"I'm here. I'm just... disappointed."

Abbie pushed her hair back from her face. "Yeah, I

know. I— Sometimes I have to work weekends to catch up, you know?"

"No, I know. But this weekend..."

Abbie said, "I gotta go. I've got a meeting. We can talk later."

"Sure."

But they didn't talk later. Abbie dodged his calls until Sunday, when she texted him saying she needed more time. If she saw him again, she would weaken again. She was falling too hard and too fast for this guy. At some point, they would have to talk of a future together in concrete terms, and someone would have to choose. Law school had been, frankly, miserable. For three years, she'd sacrificed having a life, all the while thinking of how it would be when she got that great law firm job and made partner. Giving up now would mean all of that work would have been in vain. As for Jack, he was never going to leave his dream job. It was out of the question. He loved what he did, and he loved where he did it. So it would fall on her to give up her own life and go live with this man and his dog. In time, she would grow to resent him for making her give up all this—her career.

She couldn't do it.

THE FOLLOWING WEDNESDAY, Abbie set down a box in a new office with a window. She stood and stared out at the view. This was it—everything she had worked for. She'd done it.

The phone rang. "He's what?" She hung up and stepped into the doorway. Taylor was headed her way, followed by Jack. Down the long office-lined corridor, he strode in his plaid shirt, jeans, and work boots, leaving a wake of heads popping out of doorways to watch the brawny mountain man walking away. They knew a good view when they saw one. He looked hot. Abbie couldn't deny it.

"Look who I found in the lobby!" Taylor smiled and gestured for Jack to go into the office. The three of them stood there, saying nothing. Taylor looked from one grim face to the other. "Well, I'll just be going." Taylor tiptoed out of the office.

"Nice view." Jack stepped over to the window.

"I didn't expect to see you here." She couldn't help but stare at his slightly mussed hair and strong cheekbones, with those gray eyes that, just now, looked quite sharp. Pounding heart and flushed cheeks—yes, he still had that effect on her.

"I was in the neighborhood." He turned and looked into her eyes. No one who was just in the neighborhood stared with such fierce emotion.

Everything she had thought and rehearsed in her

mind seemed to fly out that window, lost in its nice view. When his eyes bored through hers, as they were doing right now, she couldn't be held responsible for her response.

He took two steps and swept her into his arms and kissed her until her hand frantically groped the air in search of her desk for support. He released her and said, "Now tell me you don't want a future together."

She took a fortifying breath. She didn't want to talk now. She just wanted his lips on hers again. "I never said that," she managed to say.

A man in a suit walked by and stuck his head in to say, "Congratulations!"

Abbie turned, startled, but recovered with a forced smile and said, "Thanks!" Her smile was gone as quickly as it had appeared.

Jack glanced at the open box on her desk. Framed diplomas and a laptop stuck out of the top. "Congratulations?"

"I made partner." She never thought she'd say those words with so little emotion.

He nodded with a troubled expression. "You've done it. I'm happy for you."

"Jack—"

"No, I am. You've got everything you've ever wanted."

His words stung most of all because they were true.

She'd worked so hard for this—too hard to leave it behind, even for him. She wanted him, too, but it just couldn't be.

It hurt to see the pain in his eyes. "I'm sorry. I just can't see us finding enough common ground to build anything on."

"Common ground? I don't even know what you're talking about. I love you. That's all the common ground I need. But I get it. It's different for you."

How could three words feel like a stab wound? As if the wind had been knocked out of her, she couldn't speak. She wanted to tell him that she loved him, too, but that would only make it hurt more, because nothing would change. If she told him she loved him, she'd have to admit she didn't love him enough to give up her career to be with him.

Ignoring her silence, he went on, "If we loved each other, we'd be able to work it all out. It's what people do. Lives together don't just happen—they're built."

Right again. She had no argument for him.

He went to the window and then to the door, pacing as if he were caged. "I never asked for a commitment. Not yet, anyway. I'm just saying that most people fall in love and then worry about the rest later on. I've got to hand it to you—you're efficient." A bitter edge came through that she'd never heard from him.

Abbie practically whispered, "Sometimes love isn't enough."

He turned to her with a look that Abbie would never forget. While she was protecting her own heart, she'd wounded his deeply. At this moment, she knew how much she loved him, because the pain in his eyes was unbearable. She suddenly wished she could take it all back. "Jack..."

He swallowed. "I've got to go. I've got an appointment."

"An appointment?" Her heart sank. "Are you sick?" Why else would he have come into the city?

"With the National Park Service here in the city—for a job. I called in a favor with a guy at work, so it's too late to cancel."

"A job interview?" He'd done it for her, and she'd just stomped on his heart.

With a rueful chuckle, he said, "Yeah. Don't worry. I've got a suit in the car." He glanced toward the door, but his gaze was soon drawn back to her. His eyes fixed on hers long enough to finish breaking her heart. Then he said, "Congratulations for making partner." He looked down, his jaw clenched. With a quick glance at her, he turned and strode out of the office.

Abbie watched through the glass wall as he walked down the hall and out of her life.

## SEVENTEEN

"A JOB INTERVIEW in the city. I didn't see that coming." Abbie looked up from her coffee to Taylor, who met her gaze with sympathy.

"He was willing to move for you?"

Abbie exhaled. "Apparently so."

"Maybe he'll think it through and have second thoughts about your relationship. After all, getting that job could solve all of your problems."

"No, he won't. By the time he told me, I'd pretty much told him I didn't love him enough—or at all, actually."

Taylor shook her head. "Don't you think he did that on purpose—not telling you in advance? Not exactly fair, was it?"

Abbie shrugged. "I can't really blame him. It was a

perfect litmus test for whether we had what it takes, and I failed."

Taylor sat in sympathetic silence for a time then got up decisively. "I'll be right back." She returned with a rich chocolate brownie, which she proceeded to cut into bite-sized pieces. Abbie glanced at it and smiled, more to herself than to Taylor. Taylor slid the plate toward her. "C'mon... it'll make everything better. It's been scientifically proven. Don't make me call an expert witness." She made a stern face that drew a weak chuckle from Abbie.

Abbie took a piece of the brownie. "All I wanted was one perfect Christmas. Why did everything have to go so terribly wrong?"

"Maybe because there's no such thing as a perfect Christmas, or anything else. Except us," Taylor added with sparkling eyes.

"I guess you make a good point."

"That we're perfect? Uh, yeah! And that men aren't? Absolutely. My goal is to find that one imperfect man who annoys me the least. Now there's a man I could spend the rest of my life with."

She smiled to see Abbie's mood brighten.

Taylor went on. "Oh—and great sex. I'd like that, too."

Abbie's eyes teared up forlornly. She practically whimpered, "We had great sex."

Taylor said to herself, "Dang. I was doing so well."

Abbie stared at the coffee shop employee as he restocked a shelf with Valentine's Day gift mugs and chocolate. She whined, "And stupid Valentine's Day doesn't help!"

"Oh, wow. Okay. This is drastic, but have you got plans tonight?"

"Yes. I'm going to be busy not spending the evening with someone I love."

"Good. I'll bring a bottle—two bottles—of... anything, some Chinese food, and we'll binge-watch Jane Austen adaptations."

Abbie looked somewhat assuaged as she asked through her tears, "Which ones?"

"Ah, well, I categorize them by leading men. So... we could start with some Greg Wise, followed by Jeremy Northam, of course Colin Firth, and in a startling break in type from the tall, dark, and handsome heroes of every other Jane Austen adaptation I can think of, we could finish with the refreshingly blond—but angsty and fist-bite-inducing Rupert Penry-Jones."

"I think you're making a terrible mistake," Abbie said, deep in thought.

Taylor looked genuinely surprised, if not concerned.

Abbie said, "You've completely left out Matthew Macfadyen."

"Oh, you're right! An unforgivable oversight!"

"And what about Ciarán Hinds?"

Taylor slowly nodded with approval.

"And James McAvoy."

Taylor frowned. "Now, *Becoming Jane* wasn't really an adaptation, was it? As adorable as James McAvoy is, if we let that slip by, then we're opening the door to *Lost in Austen*."

Abbie's face lit up. "Yes! Bring that, too!"

By the time they'd left to return to work, Abbie had thrown the Brontës into the mix, prompting heated debate.

TIME DID NOT HEAL all wounds, at least not in four days. Abbie sat in her dark window office and shut down her computer. The last one at work on Valentine's Day, she walked down the dim hallway, rode an empty elevator down to the ground floor, and went out of the building. As she walked up the avenue, it looked as though every couple in love had come out to remind her how happy they were. It was all she could do not to curse as she passed them. Not that they didn't have a right to be happy, she conceded. But as she walked past yet another shop window with Valentine's gifts front and center, she inwardly muttered, *If I see another effing bear with a heart...*

When she arrived at her building, the doorman handed her a package. It was from Jack.

"Happy Valentine's Day!" said the doorman, who was taking the holiday better than she was.

She gave half a nod and mumbled the same. Once upstairs, she set the package down on the table. What if he'd ordered it before they last met? "O cruel fate, thou suckest."

She stared at the package for a moment or two then sat down on the edge of the sofa, took a deep breath, and tore off the brown paper. "If it's one of those bears with a heart, I swear I'll shove that little bastard down the garbage disposal."

Abbie,

You left these. No hard feelings.

Love,

Jack

P.S.— I didn't get the job, so I guess you
          were right. It wouldn't have
          worked out.

Wrapped in a few paper towels were the cookie cutters she'd left at the cabin. She'd forgotten about them. She exhaled, disappointed. "Well, what did you expect?"

She picked up the box to get it out of her sight, when she heard something bump against the side of the box. She reached in and found—also unceremoniously wrapped in a paper towel—a copper cookie cutter in the shape of a log cabin. She turned it over in her hands. He had touched it, and she felt foolish because touching it made her feel closer to him.

She recalled sitting with him by the fire, when he'd read Yeats to her. "Murmur, a little sadly, how love fled... and hid his face amid a crowd of stars."

She already felt old and full of sleep. She'd achieved her life goal. She'd made partner and continued to toil away at work that she didn't really enjoy. Since they'd parted, her thoughts had been more on Jack than on her successful career. But how many people could have it all? Life just wasn't like that.

But she'd had a chance, and she'd blown it.

Abbie sat up in bed and looked at the clock. Eleven o'clock. *Wow. Look at you, Miss Partner, living the dream.*

Then a thought nagged at her. *Is this really the life that you want?*

Jack had sent her that little cabin cookie cutter as a reminder of their week together. Why would he have done that if he didn't want her to remember? And if he wanted that, maybe there was a chance that he still wanted her.

But here they were, back where they'd left off: with him in the mountains and her in the city. But he'd tried to meet her far more than halfway. Maybe it was her turn.

She picked up her phone. "Taylor? It's Abbie."

"Is something wrong?"

"No. I'm sorry. I know it's late, but I wanted to tell you. I won't be in for the rest of the week—or maybe ever. Wish me luck."

"Luck?"

"I'm going to the mountains."

Abbie was beaming as she hung up the phone. She got out of bed and threw some clothes and toiletries into an overnight bag. She was nearly packed when she realized that she didn't have a car. She did a quick Internet search on her phone and found a twenty-four-hour car rental place across town. An hour later, she was on her way up the West Side Highway with a venti coffee in the cup holder beside her.

A little after 6:00 a.m., Abbie stood at Jack's door

and knocked. After what seemed like an eternity, the door opened, and there he stood, disheveled and wearing only his boxers.

*Oh, dammit, just take me now.*

He looked as if he thought he was dreaming. "Abbie?"

"I'm sorry I didn't call first."

He shook his head, still looking confused. "It's okay. Come in."

She followed him into the kitchen but stopped in the doorway when she spied Boomer asleep in the corner.

Jack woke Boomer up and led him to another room then returned, closing the door behind him.

Abbie said, "Taylor gave me the name of a therapist. She's supposed to be able to cure people of their fear of dogs within weeks."

"Okay." He looked even more confused.

Abbie couldn't seem to collect her thoughts. "I know I'm not making any sense." She looked about the room. "I got your package."

"Oh, that. I kept meaning to bring those to you."

"Thank you."

"Abbie... why are you here?"

"I'm quitting my job. It turns out I don't love being partner. It also turns out I love you."

Jack didn't move for a moment. "I didn't get the job. I can't leave here anytime soon."

Abbie smiled. "I know. I don't care about that. I just care about you."

"Abbie..."

She rushed into his arms and kissed him. Between kisses, he said, "Are you sure?"

"I've never been surer of anything."

Jack held her face in his hands. "It's not going to be perfect."

She looked into his eyes. "Perfect is boring."

"Abbie Harper, you will never be boring."

# EIGHTEEN

*THE FOLLOWING CHRISTMAS*

On the snow-covered lawn in front of an old log cabin stood a small wooden sign that said, Abbie Harper Whelan, Attorney at Law.

The front door swung open, and out walked a very pregnant attorney, followed closely behind by her forest ranger husband, with an overnight bag on his shoulder and a dog at his heels.

As he slipped his arm about her waist to support her, she grumbled, "But it's Christmas! This was not supposed to happen this way."

Jack steadied her as he led her down the walk to his pickup truck. "I never promised you perfect."

"Good, 'cause if you had, I'd be filing a lawsuit on the way to the hospital."

Jack smiled. "That's one of the reasons I love you. You're a great multitasker."

Her pain having subsided for the moment, she looked at him in earnest. "Do you really think so?"

"No." He laughed and helped her into the seat and buckled her in. Then he put his hand on her cheek. "But I love you." And he kissed her.

She looked up at him with a soft look in her eyes. "I love you, too." Then she moaned at the onslaught of another contraction. "Okay, you can skip the courthouse. Just get me to a hospital."

And Jack did just that, while Boomer barked his good-bye.

# THANK YOU!

Thank you for reading *The Christmas Cabin*. With so many options, I appreciate your choosing my book to read. Your opinion matters, so please consider sharing a review to help other readers.

BOOK
REVIEWS

## ACKNOWLEDGMENTS

Thank you to Colonel Andrew T. Jacob, Assistant Director of Forest Rangers, Division of Forest Protection, New York State Department of Environmental Conservation. Colonel Jacob graciously answered my questions about forest rangers with specific and helpful details, for which I am grateful. I applaud him and his department for the work that they do.

Thanks to authors Nick Russell and Billy Kring, who shared their knowledge of guns and police procedures. If either of them rents a secluded cabin in the mountains, do not park in their driveway without advance notice.

Thanks also to Ethan Gutzeit of Gtarms.com, for recommending a number of choices for Jack's off-duty weapon and for coaching me on proper firearm terminology. He actually knows a guy who could Cerakote a Glock for me in Barbie pink. (I was kidding!)

To my librarian daughter, I extend my gratitude for tirelessly listening to and advising me on my some-times-nutty plot ideas.

And finally, thanks to my personal hero, with whom I am happily stranded in our own mountain home.

NEXT

ALSO BY J.L. JARVIS

For a Reader's Guide to more books by J.L. Jarvis,

visit jljarvis.com/books.

# ABOUT THE AUTHOR

J.L. Jarvis is a left-handed opera singer/teacher/lawyer who writes romance novels. She received her undergraduate training from the University of Illinois at Urbana-Champaign and a doctorate from the University of Houston. She now lives and writes in New York.

*Sign up to be notified of book releases and related news:*
http://news.jljarvis.com

*Follow JL online at:*
Website: jljarvis.com
Facebook: facebook.jljarvis.com
Twitter: twitter.jljarvis.com
Tumblr: tumblr.jljarvis.com
Pinterest: pinterest.jljarvis.com
Bookbub: bookbub.jljarvis.com
Email: jl@jljarvis.com

Made in the USA
Columbia, SC
10 April 2019